THE WILL OF THE PEOPLE

Paul K Joyce

ACKNOWLEDGEMENTS

THE WILL OF THE PEOPLE
Paul K Joyce

The first book in:

The Will Of The People trilogy
THE WILL OF THE PEOPLE
AFTER THE FALL
THE GATHERING STORM*

My thanks to David and Shirley,
the York Tribe, CJ Flood, and especially to
David J. and my family
Cover artwork: Tom Partridge
www.paulkjoyce.com[1]

---

1. http://www.paulkjoyce.com

Prologue

The noose slipped around his neck. The crowd roared, and the air was thick with excitement. Poster boy and front-page darling, he was everyone's son or brother. Now they wanted him dead.

1. Brexit Day

'Mum—the Internet's gone off!'

Sitting at the breakfast bar, I only just heard Grace's distant shout above the din in the kitchen. Mum was grinding coffee beans, the kettle was going and some guy on the TV was getting very excited about a *breaking news* item. Mum moved across to the bread bin, blocking my view of the screen. The kettle flicked off, and she jammed three slices of bread into the toaster. It ticked, counting down.

It was time.

'What did she say?' said Mum, busy behind the fridge door.

I put down my mug of tea on the immaculately clean counter.

'Something about the Internet,' I said. I looked down at my phone, groaning inwardly when I saw the time. 'Yeah, it's not working. I've got nothing, not even 4G.'

'That's all we need,' said Mum, closing the door with her foot. 'On top of everything.'

Something hit the French doors—hard. I jumped.

'What the heck was that?' said Mum.

'No idea, a bird or something?' I said.

She shrugged her shoulders and poured steaming water into the coffee jug. It was still dark outside and white light from the kitchen spilled onto the lawn transforming it into a glittering crystal carpet. I shivered and felt the hairs on my arms and neck rising.

So, the day has finally arrived.

The melodramatic voice came from a man on the TV. He was standing outside the Houses of Parliament clutching a woolly microphone. It was frosty there too, and his red nose and constant shivering undermined his earnest expression. He looked like he could do with a hat and a hot drink.

Today, after years of disagreement and endless negotiation, the UK will leave the European Union.

'At last,' said Mum. 'We can forget about it and move on.'

My eyes flashed to the doorway to check that Dad wasn't there. It was too early for another argument. With a tea towel over her arm, Mum took several plates from the oven. In her smart grey trouser suit she looked too well dressed to be making breakfast. Why couldn't we just help ourselves, like a regular day? She furiously whisked the yellowy contents of a bowl.

'In fact,' she said. 'When I've scrambled these eggs, I think breakfast will be just about ready. Joel, give your father and sister a call, would you?'

'Sure thing, Mum.'

I arrived at the bottom of the stairs just as Dad was making his way down. Unusually, he was wearing jeans with his standard black shirt.

'Morning, son.'

'Hi, Dad. Mum said to say that breakfast is ready.'

'Great. Oh, Joel?'

'Yeah?'

'You can still come with me today, if you want to—to the STAY rally. Now you've got your test, you could drive me there if you like?'

I shook my head, trying not to show the usual rush of irritation that resulted from nearly everything he said. 'What's the point, Dad? It's all sorted, isn't it? We're leaving and that's the end of it. I just can't see what good taking to the streets will do now. Just drop it, will you?'

Dad came slowly down the last two steps and paused at the foot of the stairs, his hand resting on the polished wood bannister. He breathed out and put his other hand on my shoulder and looked me right in the eyes. Oh god, I thought, sincere moment coming up.

'You just can't think like that. This isn't over, trust me.'

He wouldn't look away, and it was a weird moment instead.

A muffled voice came from above us. 'Mum, reboot the hub, or something.'

I breathed a small sigh of relief. Dad looked up towards the top of the stairs and removed his arm.

'I'd better go up and call her,' I said.

'Okay,' said Dad. 'But the offer's there. One day out of school won't hurt, especially today.'

I gave Dad the best smile I could manage, but I think he got the message. The truth was, I'd given up on my point of view being represented. I was just part of a minority, part of the problem, at least that's how the referendum result made me feel. I ran up the stairs, two steps at a time, and knocked on Grace's door. No answer, I knocked again.

'Yeah?' came the tetchy response.

'Hey, breakfast is ready.'

Heavy footsteps, a rattle of the handle and the door flung open.

'What's up with the Wi-Fi? It's dead—busted...'

I opened my mouth to speak, but Grace was in full flow.

'So, I can't download the reference email for the European history module; there's no 4G, and it's due in today. I'm *this* close to a panic attack.'

I was listening, but slightly distracted, first by the exotic choreography of my little sister's hands and arms but mostly by her hair, which seemed to have expanded overnight. She was embracing her full Afro, and, like her mood, it was wild and full on. She was a lot better on her new meds and was coping well with school. Today, though, she didn't seem quite so calm.

'You coming down?' I said.

'Yeah, suppose so. Just getting my phone.'

She ran from one side of her room to the other, stepping over mounds of dreary grey and black clothes. She'd never have to worry about dressing for a funeral.

'See you down there,' she said.

I stopped and turned back to face her. 'Dad asked about the rally again. He just doesn't get it. He mention it to you?'

Grace paused in the doorway. Although she was a few inches shorter than me, her hair meant that she eclipsed me. A faint smell of burnt toast wafted up from downstairs.

'Yeah, but he's given up,' said Grace. 'And Mum's definitely not going.'

I gave her my super wide-eyed sarcastic look. 'Whatever gave you that idea?' I said. 'She's in a right mood.'

'And what's with the whole breakfast thing?'

'I'm not sure. I think it's Mum's way of trying to make Dad feel better about—'

'I don't even want to think about it,' said Grace. ' It just makes me so angry even hearing the word.'

'Brexit?'

She put her hands up to her ears and shook her head.

'Stop it. Don't say that word. If I don't hear it, I can almost believe it's not happening.'

Just for a second I could see that look on her face, a desperate emptiness. Like the time after the incident in the shop. It was just after the vote and she was picking some things up for Mum after school. A woman, a customer, said to the shopkeeper, right in front of Grace: 'Now we can get rid of *her* lot. She can go back where she came from.' Grace was too shocked to say anything, and the shopkeeper said precisely nothing. It really got to her. I wish I'd been there. That was the new reality: strangers in our own land. She swore me to secrecy.

Grace closed her bedroom door and followed me down the stairs. Raised voices from the kitchen stopped as we opened the door. A haze of grey smoke hovered around the toaster. Mum's mouth twisted up and I could vaguely see her teeth. She wasn't convincing anyone. Fake smile.

'Morning darling,' she said.

'Hey, Mum,' said Grace.

Mum turned away from Dad, who sat back down on his stool and rustled the newspaper in front of his face. The kitchen was super bright, and there was nowhere to hide.

'Your mother and I were just chatting,' said Dad.

Mum banged a plate down on the work surface to one side of the cooker and noisily rifled through the cutlery drawer.

'Who put the tongs there?' she said.

Dad ignored her, put the newspaper down and looked at Grace. Stared would be a more accurate description.

'Your hair, darling... it's...'

Grace stopped and tilted her head. 'Yes?'

Apart from her white shirt, she was dressed entirely in black—skirt, leggings, jacket, shoes and jumper.

'I think your father is just lost for words at the stunning good looks of his only daughter,' said Mum.

Dad cleared his throat. 'That's it, exactly. And school, they're okay with...?'

'Yes, Dad. It's all cool. My hair is the least of my problems. You know the Wi-Fi's down?'

Dad nodded, but I could tell he wasn't listening. 'Talking of school,' he said. 'I've spoken to Miss Kimberley, and she's fine with you coming to the rally with me if you want to.'

Grace grabbed a half slice of charred, buttered toast, bit into it and rolled her eyes to heaven. 'OMG, Dad; I thought we'd been through all this.' The toast crunched. 'It's today I hand in my project on political history, you know that.'

'Yes, but—'

'I mean, what's the point? Why don't you ask Mum, maybe *she* could get the time off?' Grace glanced at me and I could see that mischievous look in her eyes.

Oh god, here we go, I thought. Why, Grace, why? Mum paused with two plates full of toast, scrambled eggs and tomatoes.

'Your father knows exactly my feelings on that subject.' Mum's lips pinched into an S shape and she thrust one plate in front of Dad and the other in front of me. 'I'm going to work as if it's just an ordinary day. If some people can't accept what's happening, then that's up to them.'

The same old preamble into the same old argument. I should start a blog. Grace, elbow on the counter, rested her chin on the heel of her palm. Dad cut up his toast with unnecessary vigour, using it to pile as much egg onto his fork as was humanly possible. He breathed in.

'Fine,' he said. 'If that's the way you want to play it, then so be it.' He put the fork into his mouth, and his eyes settled on the paper.

I looked at Grace, who was already firing silent questions at me with her eyes.

Had Dad given in? Maybe, after all the protests, emails and letters, even he had to admit defeat and that there would be no second referendum, no People's Vote: no undoing what had been done.

Mum put down plates for herself and Grace, steam rising from the colourful display. She kept her eyes on Dad the whole time, but he continued to chew his food without looking up. Mum sat down. 'Okay, well then, I hope everyone enjoys their breakfasts.' She bowed her head and clasped her hands. She said the usual words about being grateful for what we were about to receive. Dad paused for a moment in half-hearted acknowledgment.

'Thanks, Mum,' said Grace. 'But—'

I held up my hand. 'Hold on, there's something on the TV.' I turned up the sound.

...police are standing by as counter demonstrations are expected to disrupt today's official STAY rallies. Tensions are running high, and there's been speculation that the military may be deployed to maintain order. Up to a million people are expected to take to the streets in opposition to the formal Brexit declaration this afternoon. Communications are being hampered by serious problems with the Internet. In addition to the failed 4G network, BT has confirmed that parts of the Midlands, Scotland and the South of England are without a connection. A cold front seems to have enveloped the whole of...

'Oh my god, that is so typical,' said Grace.

'No using the Lord's name in vain,' said Mum, without looking away from Dad. She flicked the corner of his paper. He lowered his head and gave her an imperious raised-eyebrow glare.

'I did tell you that Grace had her big project today,' she said.

'Yes, I know,' said Dad. 'But this is, *comment on dire*, unprecedented.'

He split the word up, his French accent suddenly pronounced.

'So, no Internet, then?' said Grace, looking as if she was struggling to keep a lid on things. 'That's it?'

'Dad,' I said. 'Do you think it's safe to go into Nottingham, I mean, on the rally? You heard what the guy said.'

Dad swallowed and rested his knife and fork on the side of his plate.

'I have no choice,' he said. He paused and breathed in. 'I feel it is my duty.'

Mum scraped the bottom of her plate with her knife and skewered a triangle of toast with her fork before dabbing at a pool of tomato juice.

'But I heard there are pro-Brexit gangs roaming the streets,' I said. 'And the police are allowing it.'

Dad's face became an expressionless mask. 'They should be stopped.'

'Not even 4G,' said Grace. 'I'll bet the government's behind this.'

Mum's knife and fork continued to move industriously around her plate. 'Never mind all that conspiracy stuff,' she said. 'Let's just eat, can we? It's going to be a long day.'

'Is it the hub, Dad?' said Grace.

'Isn't there any bacon?' I said.

Mum gave me a steady, glassy look. 'We're trying to support Grace—remember?'

I breathed out through my nose and stared at my sister. She gave me a look, which instantly wound me up.

'Well, I don't see why I should suffer,' I said.

'Suffer?' said Dad. 'Come on, son. It's just breakfast. I'm sure they'll have bacon at school if you want it that badly.' He gulped his coffee. 'Actually, even at the restaurant we're finding more and more people are asking for vegetarian food.'

'But you're French, Dad,' I said. 'You think mince is vegetarian.'

'Ha ha,' said Dad.

'Dad, what about the hub?' said Grace, her voice a little-girl whine.

'Sorry, chérie,' said Dad. 'But I don't think it's the hub. Didn't you hear what the man said? It's all over the country.'

Grace pulled a face and set her phone face down on the counter. 'But I need that email to finish my report.'

'I know, sweetie,' said Mum, 'but what can *we* do? Let's just eat. You've worked so hard on it, I'm sure you've done more than enough.'

Grace went quiet and looked down at her food. The voice of the reporter filled the silence. She picked up her fork. It felt like the last supper.

'Just for the record, the rally starts at midday,' said Dad. He twisted the black pepper pot over his plate, showering his scrambled egg with small irregular particles. He cut into his toast and scooped up a portion. 'It's a shame we can't do this as a family.'

'Oh, for goodness' sake, Henri,' said Mum. 'Give it a rest. They're not going— I'm not coming either and that's that. Why can't you, just for once, accept that you're not going to get your way on this?'

Mum's eyes were wide and judging from the storm of words brewing on Dad's lips, she'd penetrated his newfound reserve. He wiped the corners of his mouth on his napkin, cleared his throat and started waving his knife up and down. Oh dear, lecture time.

'It's not just about opposing our leaving,' he said. 'We have to try to stop these ludicrous trade deals and alliances. Have you noticed it's mainly authoritarian bully boy regimes that we're dealing with now?'

I cleared my throat and poured myself a half mug of tea.

'Great breakfast, Mum, thanks.' I said.

Dad wasn't giving up.

'All this rhetoric about *family values* and *tradition*. I'm telling you, it's a slippery slope.' He took a breath. 'And as for Europe, we will *never* have a trading relationship with them if we align ourselves with these undemocratic nationalists. What happened to socialism, to collective bargaining?'

Grace pulled her fork from between her lips and chewed slowly, looking determinedly at her plate. Mum rolled her eyes before smiling at me.

'You're welcome, love.' She put her hand to her mouth and gave a small cough. 'Maybe if we could focus on how things *are* rather than how things might be, then we could all move on.'

Dad stopped chewing, and his eyes locked on Mum. Then, something like the sound of angry flies distracted his attention. He touched Grace's arm. 'Take those out at the table, young lady.'

Grace removed an earphone and raised her eyebrows. 'What?'

'I said… oh, it doesn't matter.' Dad shook his head. 'I feel very strongly about this and would appreciate some engagement, if not some support.'

Grace looked at Mum, then back to Dad and put her earphone back in.

The Prime Minister said this morning that he was confident that our new friends and alliances would make the UK great again.

'Are they all over there?' said Grace, leaning to get a better view of the TV screen. 'You know, the government—in Europe.'

'You're shouting, darling,' said Mum.

Grace removed both earphones.

'Soz.'

'Yeah, I think so,' I said, mopping up the last of my tomato juice.

Dad leaned back and folded his arms. 'All the heads of State have to be in Brussels to sign the final exit agreement.'

'Another jolly for the Royals,' I said.

'Joel, you almost sound political,' said Dad.

'Yeah, maybe.'

'Some of the students are staging a mock funeral, today,' said Grace. 'The headteacher tried to stop it but it's happening anyway.'

'They're too lenient at that school,' said Mum. 'In my day, we'd never have got away with something like that.'

'Really, Mum?' I said. 'I thought you were a fully signed up black rights' activist at University?'

'That was different,' said Mum.

'How was it different?' said Dad, leaning forward with his coffee cup in his hand. 'I see it as the same thing—groups of people being demonised and made to feel like aliens. It's called racism.'

'Yes, but today it's about economics... sovereignty—not colour,' said Mum.

'Are you sure?' said Dad.

Maybe I'd had too much tea, but the temperature was definitely rising. If only Mum and Dad knew about the incident with Grace in the shop. Mum glared at Dad.

'As a second-generation Black woman,' said Dad, 'I still can't believe you voted the way you did.'

There it was—the fact that dare not speak its name—the elephant in the room. Mum looked at me and then at Grace. She spoke, her voice breathy and impassioned.

'Here we go again, why do you always have to—'

'Stop it, all of you,' shouted Grace. 'I can't cope with this, not at home. It's bad enough at school, you have no idea what it's like—none of you.'

She threw down her napkin, picked up her phone and ran out of the kitchen slamming the door behind her.

Along with the entire UK government, The Queen is seen here with senior figures from the EU. The Royal family is present to witness this historic moment. Rumoured to be joining them is Prince—

Dad grabbed the remote and aimed it at the TV, pressing down hard on the red button. The weird thing was that the picture disappeared just before his finger connected with the button. He stared at the blank screen for a moment and then carried on as if nothing had happened. The sequence of events and Dad's expression only became significant, later.

2. Snow

Breakfast was over. Mum grabbed plates and stacked them, noisily. 'I thought we were trying to avoid things like this happening,' she said.

'We're treading on eggshells the whole time,' said Dad. 'We have to be able to have normal discussions.'

'Of course we do,' said Mum, standing up. 'But these aren't just discussions, are they? They're arguments, and they always come back to these fundamental issues of class and race.'

Oh god, it's really going to kick off now, I thought.

'Well, forgive me for addressing the most important subjects facing us all at this critical time in this nation's history,' said Dad.

He poured himself another coffee.

'And that's the whole point,' said Mum. 'Grace just doesn't feel as if she fits in. You know exactly what the psychiatrist said.'

'But she's seventeen and this has been going on for years. She gets better; she relapses; she gets better... it's never ending.'

'Keep your voice down,' said Mum. 'She'll hear you.'

Dad banged the coffee pot onto the counter. 'Oh, she's probably got those blessed ear things in. She can add hearing loss to her problems.'

'Oh, you're impossible sometimes,' said Mum, opening the dishwasher.

'She needs to get away from here,' I said. 'You know, go to University and be with other mixed-race kids.'

They both looked at me as if they'd just discovered that I existed. Their initial, *how dare you* look, softened.

'I suppose you're right, son,' said Dad. 'None of us could have predicted how things would change.'

'Well, I don't have any problems,' said Mum, clicking the dishwasher door shut.

'Yes, but you're a solicitor—a professional woman,' said Dad. 'It's different for you. You command respect.'

Mum lowered her head and looked at Dad through her eyebrows. I felt the familiar spark of Dad's Gallic temperament and Mum's fiery Caribbean genes. Nothing like a bit of stereotyping on a bitter Brexit morning.

'I should go up and see if she's okay,' said Dad.

I stood up and grabbed up my mug. The phone in Dad's study rang. Its distinctive chirrup made him look up. It stopped and then started again.

'Henri?' said Mum.

Dad dropped his paper and jumped up from the table.

'It's alright,' I said. 'I'm going up, anyway.'

The door to the study slammed.

Mum smiled through a heavy frown. 'You're a good brother.'

'Aw, shucks Mom,' I said, trying to hide the rush of blood to my cheeks as I stood up.

I climbed the stairs, aiming for three steps at a time but not quite achieving it. Sounds of movement from Grace's room stopped as I neared the door. I knocked.

'Hey, you okay in there?'

There was a muffled sniff.

'Yeah, I'm fine. I'm coming out now.'

'You sure you're okay?'

'Honestly,' said Grace.

'Alright then.'

I went to the bathroom and brushed my teeth, studying my face in the mirror as I reached every tooth. Would I fit in at Oxford? Was Physics the right choice? Did I like my hair this short? Or did I keep it like this to avoid standing out—raising my profile? I was glad that I was well built—strong. Maybe I should ask Sophie Laing out on a proper date? At school, most people were fine with me except for this one guy, Mitchell Stark, who was causing me big R.I.P. A shout from downstairs made me pause but all I heard were Grace's footsteps on the stairs. I spat into the bowl, picked up my phone and headed for Grace's room. Her door was open, and I could hear her and Mum's voices coming from downstairs. Mum came to the bottom of the stairs.

'You ready, Joel? We're about to head off.'

I bounced down the stairs, sticking to one step at a time. Grace stood with Mum behind her. For a moment, in the shadow of the hall I could see both their faces. They looked so alike. I'd never noticed it so clearly before. Dad joined us. His mouth was pinched and his eyebrows tight and low.

'Everything alright, darling?' said Mum.

'What? Oh yes, everything's fine.'

Even I didn't believe him, but Mum didn't seem inclined to push it. Keys jangled in her coat pocket. She touched the lapel of Grace's jacket, her fingers playing over its neatly stitched edges, smoothing and rearranging.

'We didn't mean to upset you, darling. It's just that it's an emotional time at the moment and feelings are running high.'

Grace looked up, her eyes meeting Mum's. She nodded. Mum raised her eyebrows and breathed out through her nose.

'Well, then. Hope you two have a good day.'

'Yeah, you too, Mum,' I said. Dad wasn't listening.

For a moment we were all in the hall, standing close to each other. The space didn't seem big enough to hold all our unspoken feelings. Arms were pushed into big coats, and Grace swathed herself in a trailing scarf. With his hand on the lock of the front door, Dad paused. He turned and looked at each of us.

'This is going to be a momentous day,' he said. He swallowed, and were his lips trembling a little? 'Whatever happens, I want you to know that... I love you—all of you, very much.'

Before we could react, he opened the door and an arctic blast of air instantly blew away any sentimental notions.

'Oh, wow,' said Grace.

'They weren't joking about a cold snap,' I said.

Mum took Dad's arm. The cold must have made her eyes water.

'Joel, darling,' she sniffed. 'Are you going to be warm enough? Put your beanie on.'

'I'm fine, Mum,' I said, rolling my eyes. But I was too busy trying to understand Dad's proclamation. He never said things like that.

We moved out onto the icy path leading the short distance to the road. Thick cloud held the dawn at bay, and streetlights pooled orange along the whitened, empty street. Hedges and gardens were rigid with frost. Our nice, neat house was on a nice, neat cul-de-sac in a boring part of the city.

'Right,' said Mum. 'See you later. You finish early, don't you?'

'Yeah, just after lunch,' I said.

Dad pressed his key fob, and the white-encrusted car blinked into life.

'Mum?' said Grace, putting her thumbnail between her teeth.

'Yes, darling?'

Breaths ballooned white and extravagant in the still air.

'I'm out of my Celexa tablets'

Mum stopped.

'Don't give me that look,' said Grace.

'But—'

'You don't know what it's like trying to get supplies at the moment. I'd just tracked some down before the Internet crashed.'

Dad sighed, and his eyes said, *I told you so.*

Mum shook her head. 'I just wish you'd said something earlier...' continuing as Grace's mouth opened. 'But it's not a problem.' She raised a hand. 'I'll pick them up. I assume it's from somewhere in town?'

Grace nodded. 'The pharmacy on Queen Street.'

'Okay,' said Mum.

'It won't matter if you miss a day,' said Dad, sounding more like himself.

Grace's jaw flexed.

'Yes, don't worry, love,' said Mum.

Grace lifted her chin and shook her head. 'I'm fine.'

I knew she'd missed more than a day.

'They're closing early, because of the rally,' said Grace.

'That's fine,' said Mum. 'I'll get them on the way in.'

'Come on,' I said. 'It's too cold to be standing around.'

Grace pulled her scarf up to cover her mouth. We made our way by the side of the car towards the dense yellow light of the street. The dark sky hung like a thick, grey blanket. Dad started the engine. A cloud of whitish vapour spewed from the rear of the car. He re-emerged with a plastic scraper. His fingers brushed against Grace's arm. 'Darling, I... I hope your project goes well.'

Grace's stifled reply sounded like *thanks.* Dad began scraping the ice off the windscreen as a small clump of white crystals sailed by my face on a collision course with the ground.

'Hey, I think it's snowing,' I said. 'It's a sign.'

'They didn't forecast this. I hope it doesn't settle,' said Mum.

She sat in the passenger seat and wound the window down. Dad reversed slowly out of the drive, the car enveloped by clouds of sweet-smelling mist.

'Come and meet me in town, after school,' said Mum.

Grace shrugged.

'Half-past three? We could meet at Angelo's.'

Mum was pressing Grace's buttons.

'Come on. It's a Friday. We used to do this a lot.'

Grace's head moved, building towards a full nod. 'Okay, Mum. Yeah, why not. See you there.'

That was unexpected, I thought.

'You too, Joel,' said Mum.

I thought about Sophie. What if she said *yes*? How would Mum and Dad react? Grace didn't like her.

'Joel?' said Mum.

I breathed out. 'Sounds like a plan.'

'I need to get going.' Dad's muffled voice was edgy and impatient.

'And I'll cook something special tonight,' said Mum. 'Just the four of us.'

I smiled and nodded but didn't fancy a meal where the only topic would be, could be: Brexit—especially when Dad was *so* not open to other viewpoints. Grace stood, watching increasing numbers of flakes land on her black mittens.

'We could build a snowman,' she said, and for a moment, her eyes widened and she seemed free of everything.

The car shot out of the drive and I could make out Mum's constructed smile and a hand waving furiously behind the misted-up window. Dad didn't look back. Further down the road, another car sat with its headlights blazing, but in every other house, curtains were drawn and there were no signs of life or activity. It was a great feeling, almost like having the world to yourself.

'Come on,' said Grace, 'It would be weird if we missed the bus.'

I looked at my phone: nothing.

'Yeah, coming.'

I shoved my hands in my pockets, slung my bag further over my shoulder and skidded towards my sister. I knew better than to mention the meds and kept the subject matter light.

'Are they really staging a mock funeral?' I said.

'Yeah, it's cool isn't it? Miss Kimberley even helped get some lightweight wood for the coffin. She's sick.'

'Agreed,' I said. 'Our lot are playing it safe, although I can think of quite a few people who are actually going to enjoy today, you know, going to rub it in big time.'

'We talking about that Stark guy by any chance?'

'Yep. Him and his cronies, and some of the teachers too. Fascists—all of them. They've been giving me a hard time for years, although they've never been able to come and out and say anything directly.'

'Until now,' said Grace, her voice almost a whisper. The snow had lost its magic.

We were leaving faint footprints in the thin canopy of white. We turned from the relative calm of the suburbs onto the main road and alongside queuing traffic, belching exhausts and fierce car tail lights.

'Needn't have worried about the bus, it's going to be late, anyway,' I said.

Grace pulled her scarf back up over her nose. A wind was getting up and it was bitingly cold.

'What do you think was up with Dad?' I said.

'He really wound me up,' said Grace.

'I know, but I meant when we were leaving.'

'You mean all the *love* stuff?'

'Well, yeah.'

'Guilty conscience.'

'Really?' I said. 'Did you see his face? I think he meant it.'

'I don't know what to think any more,' said Grace.

A cut-glass voice came from behind us.

'Hey, guys.'

I turned and there she was—Sophie Laing. She was running to catch up, her long blonde hair caught by the breeze. She wore a light denim top, off her shoulders, over a collared polka-dot shirt. Below her short black skirt a tantalising area of tanned thigh was visible, interrupted by above-the-knee leggings. Her slender legs culminated in purple high-heel boots. A foot shorter than me, she was a walking ray of sunshine—a sweet I wanted to unwrap.

'Oh, hi, Sophie,' said Grace, tilting her head and pulling her scarf away from her mouth. She looked at me, and her eyes widened. 'What a coincidence? Isn't it nice to bump into Sophie, Joel, for what is it, the third time this week?'

'That many?' said Sophie, flakes lodging on her long lashes. Perfect makeup accentuated the crystal blue of her eyes. I breathed in her familiar fruity perfume.

'Yeah, I think it really is,' said Grace, the corners of her mouth twitching.

'Anyway,' I said. 'Aren't you cold?'

'Oh, Dad, like, gave me a lift to the junction back there, and it's not that far to the bus.' Her voice rose at the end of every sentence.

'There's going to be a bit of a wait with all this traffic,' I said. I took off my beanie and held it out to her. 'This will keep your head warm, at least.'

'No, I—'

'Go on, I insist.'

Grace folded her arms and Sophie showed her teeth, but not in any way that could be considered a smile. The beanie was actually too big, and she looked around to see if anyone was watching. She kept pushing her hair back and slipping her hand under the material.

'Thanks,' she said. 'That's... kind.'

The bus stop was no more than a sign by a large, leafless tree. Other kids milled around, heads down. Further along the road, a group of huddled figures were smoking, using their lapels as wind breaks. I couldn't say much to Sophie with Grace standing between us, and she showed no signs of moving.

'What's going on with the Internet?' I said.

'Yeah, it's kind of like, weird,' said Sophie. 'I've got nothing.'

Grace sighed. Snow continued to fall.

'So, how are things?' I said, moving from one foot to the other in a vain attempt to warm up.

'Oh, fine,' said Sophie.

Just feet away from us, cars inched forwards. There was no sign of the bus.

'Cool,' I said.

The traffic lights changed to green, and the cars began to move. I could see a bus in the distance. 'Your mum and dad, they're well?'

'Oh, for god's sake,' said Grace. 'I think I'll go and talk to Georgia Martin.'

She stomped off, almost slipping over. She recovered—just.

'Was it, like, something I said?' said Sophie.

I shook my head. 'Nah, she's just stressed.'

Sophie looked up at me. The wind and snow conspired to make us as uncomfortable as possible. We both began speaking at the same time.

'Joel, I was...'

'Maybe we could...'

We laughed. I liked the way my name sounded on her lips.

'No, you go first,' I said.

She moved strands of hair from her face. Her nose was bright pink. I wanted to kiss her.

'I was just wondering if, like, you know...'

The bus pulled up with a hiss of brakes, and the doors opened. A scrum of insistent bodies jostled around us.

'Sorry, what?' I said.

A girl pushed between us.

Sophie shook her head. 'It doesn't matter.'

She got on the bus before me. I wanted to sit next to her, to feel the warmth of her leg against mine, but there were no double seats left and the nearest I could get to her was three rows nearer the back. I sat next to a mousy-haired girl with thin lips. The bus was super warm, which was some compensation. Grace was making her way towards me.

'Your girlfriend run off with someone else, then?' she said, leaning down and nudging my shoulder.

'She's not my girlfriend,' I said, my eyes attempting to register innocence and disdain.

'Good.'

I knew she didn't think much of Sophie. She'd never said anything, but I saw the sour looks whenever her name was mentioned or we met at the bus stop. Maybe Sophie was superficial, and a bit of a tease, but something happened when she looked at me; I felt strong—alive. It was a great feeling. The bus jerked away from the kerb and our heads bobbed around like chastised dolls. The mood was different today. No one was talking, or if they were, it was muted. The roar and steady vibration of the engine seemed like a good excuse not to engage with the world for half an hour. Sophie took off the beanie, shook her hair out and pulled her fingers through any remaining tangles. I could make out the delicate curve of her neck. She looked round and smiled. I smiled back. My dick was bursting out of my pants and no amount of shifting and careful wriggling seemed to help. I hoped thin-lips next to me didn't notice. If we had to evacuate the bus, I'd be in real trouble.

The driver put his radio on and music burst through the thick, warm air, followed by a series of adverts. I now knew where to get the best deal on car tyres and who to use to sort out a PPI claim. In the next song, after a cheesy introduction, the singer told us that *things... can only get better.* I assumed it was the DJ's attempt at irony. Sure enough, a sickeningly smarmy voice did the link from hell into the next, Brexit-themed ditty. My trouser situation was sorted.

Through the misted-up windows and above the glare of car brake lights and streetlights, the first glimmer of light in the sky was just becoming visible. Breaks appeared in the thick snow clouds, with clear sky in places. I looked at my phone. Still no 4G. I drummed my fingers on the leather seat. Usually I'd game for the whole journey. Grace was scribbling something and looking intelligent. I could still only see the back of Sophie's head. A serious-sounding man's voice interrupted the music. It said something about a confirmed pro-Brexit counter-rally in the city and warned about the possibility of violent clashes. The police were advising people to leave the city immediately after the rally.

A cold feeling began in my stomach. Would Dad and Mum be okay? Should we be meeting in town? If we didn't, Grace wouldn't get her meds. I looked at my phone again. No signal. I closed my eyes and ordered my heart to stop pounding. I conjured Dad's face as we stood in the hall. There was something about his eyes that told me he meant every word that he said. I couldn't put a name to the feeling that began in my stomach and seeped upwards through my chest.

My hand draped over the side of the boat into the cool, clear water. I marvelled at how the sea endlessly captured and redistributed the light—flickering, mesmeric. The shore, a distant shimmering green, carried voices and laughter and there was time, so much time. Something knocked against the wooden hull.

3. School

I twitched and opened my eyes. The snow-covered pillars of the school gates floated by and we bumped over something in the road. I sat up as the bus manoeuvred past snow-free parked cars and made its way to the far end of the car park. The engine shuddered and stopped. In the sudden and unnatural calm we shuffled off the bus. Everyone seemed subdued, speaking in hushed tones or not saying anything at all. Grace kept her head down. Sophie got off before me and was chatting to the other posh girls, their haw-haw laughter sparking prickles of irritation. I didn't relate to them. I tried to catch Sophie's eye, but she didn't turn round.

The dawn was imminent. Snow covered every building, and I felt an almost childish feeling of delight. It didn't last long. Something hard and cold hit the back of my head. I turned around and Mitchell Stark and his mates were standing, laughing. Despite the weather, Stark wasn't wearing a jacket, and the knot of his tie was halfway down his not-quite-white shirt. He was shorter than the rest, with a stocky build and a radical haircut.

'Know what day it is, monkey boy?' he shouted, his voice a thick, northern sore-throat rasp.

I flicked chunks of snow off the back of my jacket and shoulder and carried on walking. I'd heard it all before.

'The day everyfing changes,' he said.

His cronies bared their knuckles and muttered assent. Out of nowhere, Sophie took my arm. The warmth and strength of the gesture took me by surprise. She glanced over at her friends and multiple camera flashes flickered in the icy gloom. She turned and looked up at me, her eyes sparkling. A chorus of high-pitched siren *oooohs* sprang from my tormentors.

Grace's voice came from behind me. 'Don't say anything to them, they are so not worth it.' She walked close behind, clutching her books to her chest.

'Give him a banana,' shouted one of the gang, his face hidden under his hoodie. His shoulders lowered, and he shifted his weight from each bent leg to the other. Wild laughter followed, and several of them pushed each other, doubled over with hysterics. My teeth clamped together and my hands balled into fists. Sophie tightened her grip around my arm. We slowed a little but had momentum.

'Just ignore them,' she said.

'Save a bit for his psycho sister, though.'

I didn't see who said it. All I saw was a finger make a circular motion near their temple. I stopped. The world turned red and something took over my mind and muscles—an unstoppable force. A scream came from behind me but all I saw was the blur of slush-covered concrete beneath my feet and the looks on the faces of the gang, almost in slow motion as my fist headed towards and made contact with Mitchell Stark's grinning face.

It was a soup of bodies and rage. I was on top of Stark, my arm raised for another strike. A sudden pain in my side made me stop and between bared teeth and spittle I saw Sophie's anguished face shaking from side to side. She was saying something but the roaring in my head drowned everything out.

I was lifted up, pulled bodily from the depths and raised to my feet. Someone was saying my name. Snowflakes continued to fall from the sky.

'Durand. Are you listening to me? Joel? Joel. Stop this, now.'

It was a man's voice. I stopped trying to pull away and focussed. The man's mouth was moving and I realised it was Mr Grant, the physics teacher.

'What? Sir, I'm sorry, I...'

Other teachers and students stood close by, watching. Stark was leaning against one of his mates, his hand covering his nose.

'He started it, sir,' he shouted. 'Fucking wog.'

Mr Grant turned away from me, and in an athletic move, reached Stark and grabbed his lapels. He seemed to float towards the teacher's face. Mr Grant looked like he was going to hit him.

'You've gone too far this time, Stark,' he said. 'Headteacher's office, now. You'll be suspended for this.'

Stark's face twisted in grim, fleshy defiance. There was blood smeared under his nose and across one cheek. His dark eyebrows lowered and his upper lip curled to show teeth set in vivid red gums.

'You touched me. It's assault, Sir,' he said, spitting out the last word with icy venom. 'They all saw you.' He wiped his mouth with the sleeve of his shirt, creating a red smear across the white polyester.

Mr Grant shoved him away and stood completely still, holding him in a heavy stare. 'Forget it, Stark. You're not getting away with it this time.'

The wind whipped the snow into a vortex around us, and for a moment, Mr Grant stood between me, Sophie and Grace on one side and Stark's mob on the other. Around us, the whole school seemed to have gathered: silent witnesses. Lights in the classrooms blazed, and the night seemed reluctant to give up the moon. When I moved, my side was tender.

'That's it, break it up,' said Mr Green, the geography teacher. 'Stark, you heard what Mr Grant said. Headteacher's office, now.' He turned to me. 'You'll have to go too, Joel.' He registered my expression. 'I know, but the Head will have to hear both sides of what happened.'

'Yes, sir,' I said.

Sophie took my hand and turned it over. There was reassurance in her eyes.

'You've grazed your knuckles.'

'I hit him as hard as I could.'

'It's alright,' said Grace, inserting herself between us. 'I'll take it from here.'

Sophie held up both hands. 'Hey. I was just, like, trying to be supportive.'

Grace ignored her and turned to me. 'Thanks for... you know, not letting them get away with saying those things.'

I shook my head. 'I just lost it,' I said. It wasn't a good feeling. I felt dirty, somehow, and my side was aching.

'Nice one,' said a boy from class. 'He had it coming.'

I shivered.

'We should go in,' said Grace.

'I could stay with you?' said Sophie.

'Well...' said Grace, her face registering irritation.

I raised my eyebrows.

Grace sighed. 'Okay, yeah. Of course.'

Once inside the main doors, the heat seemed to revive me. Meltwater trickled down the back of my neck. Grace unpicked her layers of clothing, beginning with her scarf. The main entrance was busy and noisy. Everyone seemed to get on with their day, except it didn't feel like an ordinary day. A nervous tension, like static, crackled in the air. There was no sign of Stark or any of the others. Mr Grant handed me a piece of paper.

'The Head will see you after the first lesson, he's tied up until then.'

'Okay, sir.'

'Off the record, that Stark boy is going to get what's coming to him.'

'Yes, sir.'

He half smiled. 'Fill in that incident form and bring it with you. And don't worry, you won't see him, or his so-called friends—they've been taken out of class.'

I nodded. He turned and headed towards the main corridor.

'Who knew he was a human being?' said Grace.

The first bell rang.

'Better get moving,' I said. My hand jerked to the source of the pain.

'You okay?' said Grace.

'Yeah, I think one of them must have kicked me or something, it's tender, that's all.'

Grace narrowed her eyes. 'See you at lunch?'

'Sure, if I'm not expelled.'

'Ha ha.' Her smile disappeared when she glanced at Sophie.

'Come on,' said Sophie. 'Better not keep Miss Talland waiting.'

Grace headed off, looking back only once as Sophie took my arm, which, thanks to my sister, now felt like a guilty pleasure. What was her problem?

A commotion coming from the toilets opposite distracted me. The door flew open, and Stark blew out, shadowed by two of his entourage. The bitter tang of disinfectant followed them.

'Come on, you three,' said Mr Grant, just behind them. 'No dawdling.' He pushed Stark's shoulder, but he seemed glued to the floor. A plaster covered the bridge of his bulging nose; the puffy skin around it a riot of emergent reds, blues and greens. His eyes drilled into mine.

'You better watch your back.'

Mr Grant grabbed his shirt and pulled him away. His mates followed, more sheep than wolves. Miss Talland appeared, a stack of books heavy in both arms. Sophie let go of me.

Miss Talland was new. She was tall with red hair and had a penchant for colourful trousers. Apart from these serious flaws, there was something about her that was really likeable. I tried to return Sophie's smile as we took our seats, but my eyes were drawn to the phone resting on my lap. No signal. I bit into my knuckle, rolling the loose skin between my teeth.

Miss Talland was out of breath. 'Crikey, the traffic was terrible this morning, wasn't it?' she said. 'I was sure I was going to be even later. And the weather—as if things weren't... ' She made a small cough and scanned the class before putting her car keys on her desk and pulling a large folder out of her briefcase. 'Better keep off that subject,' she said, more to herself than to us.

Sophie sat in her usual place near the front and next to her friend, Charlotte. Giggly, silly, Charlotte kept checking her phone, looking around and smirking at me until Sophie nudged her. I wasn't in the mood.

Miss Talland clapped her hands, stood up very straight and ran her fingers through her hair. She pitched her voice at a: *you will listen to me and do everything I say,* intensity.

'As you all know,' she began. 'Today is a day like no other.'

Everyone began muttering and talking again. Miss Talland held up her hands and the hubbub subsided.

'Thank you,' she said. 'And in honour of this momentous occasion, we're going to revisit another seminal moment in British history.'

Dylan Sutton raised his hand. 'Do you mean like in fluid, Miss?' he said, ducking down and pulling a mouth-open face to his friends who developed manic but suppressed giggling fits.

'Very clever, Sutton. But in a manner of speaking, yes, I do,' said Miss Talland, putting both hands on her desk and leaning towards us.

Sutton stopped smiling and sank into his seat. The corners of Miss Talland's mouth curved up momentarily.

'I am of course talking about the English Civil War, which tore this country apart between sixteen forty-two and sixteen fifty-one. You see, Sutton, it was King Charles the First's marriage to Henrietta Maria, a Catholic princess, that set this country on the path to war.'

Sutton stared at her. 'Yes, Miss.'

Miss Talland continued with the build up to the execution of Charles the First. I stopped listening. Sophie turned around and smiled. I remembered the multiple flashes as she took my arm—the knowing looks. A bitter taste swirled at the back of my throat.

There was a knock at the classroom door, and the school secretary walked in. She was smartly dressed, but it was the clutched handkerchief and her red eyes that held my attention. She mumbled an apology and walked over to the desk.

'Open your books at page forty-three, class, and read the first two paragraphs,' said Miss Talland.

A ripple of hushed murmurs spread through the class as the woman whispered in Miss Talland's ear. As she listened, her expression changed, and her hand went up to her mouth. She looked at the older woman as if to seek clarification. The woman nodded. I could see Miss Talland's lips, mouth: *oh my god*. She looked at us and then back at the woman. I thought about Mum and Dad. The woman's bottom lip quivered. Everyone was silent, looking forward. Miss Talland cleared her throat as the other woman turned and headed towards the door, head down. She moved from behind her desk and put a splayed hand on its polished surface. Her face was drained of colour.

My phone buzzed: a missed call from Mum. It vibrated a second time and there was a two-word text message—from Dad this time: *I'm sorry*. I read it again and held my breath. There wasn't time to think. Miss Talland was speaking.

'Class,' she said. 'You need to listen to me very carefully.' She swallowed. 'Something has—'

The lights went out.

4. Fracture

It was perfectly dark and, for a moment, utterly silent. Someone screamed and questioning voices erupted. Phone lights came on and the room filled with dancing shadows. A distant bell sounded, and dull red lights on the ceiling sprang into life.

We had descended into hell. *I'm sorry... I'm sorry...* Dad's message raced around my head.

'Everybody stay calm,' shouted Miss Talland, sounding anything but calm. Her voice cracked. 'The backup generator should come on any second.'

Raised voices and the scrape of wood against wood filled the sterile space. My legs didn't want to obey commands and my throat felt tight.

'You have to stay here, in the classroom,' shouted Miss Talland. 'You can't go out.'

'What do you mean, can't go out?' said a girl's voice from the shadows. 'What's happening?'

Other voices joined in, demanding an explanation.

'Is this a joke?' said one.

Miss Talland was groping for something in her bag. She pulled out her phone and swiped to turn on the torch. It briefly illuminated her car keys on the desk beside her. She shone the light on her face. Lit from below, her eyes were black, ghoulish sockets. It was a horror movie.

'Listen to me, all of you. I'm sorry, but this isn't a drill, or a joke.' Her voice wobbled. She cleared her throat. 'Something... something has happened.'

I'm sorry. I'm sorry for what? I thought. There were no bars on my phone, but I had to try. I texted Dad: *what's happening* and pressed send: *message failed* popped up immediately. A cold feeling began in my legs and worked its way up my body—a cold, hungry anxiety ready to devour me. I made fists and breathed through my nose. The feeling subsided a little.

'What the fuck's going on, Miss?' said Ben Jackson. I could hear the naked fear in his voice.

Sophie was at my side. Her hand found mine. It had lost some of its warmth but I squeezed it anyway and in the erratic darkness I could just make out her eyes—like blue jewels. Miss Talland spoke, her head shaking from side to side.

'There's been some sort of attack. I don't know much more than that. It's affected power stations and transport. We've been told that, for the moment, everyone has to stay where they are.'

There was pandemonium. Urgent voices competed for attention. It was a tidal wave of sound.

'Is it terrorists, Miss?'

'What the fuck?'

'Is that why the power's down?'

'And the Internet?'

'Look, I don't know, I just don't know,' shouted Miss Talland, her face distorting as it caught the garish light from her phone. 'I can't answer anything if you all talk at once.'

'What about the city?' I shouted. 'The rally?' But my voice was lost in the mayhem.

'I'm frightened,' said an unidentified voice from the back. 'I want to go home.' The voice disintegrated into sobs. The emotion was contagious.

I forced myself to stay calm. I told myself that Mum and Dad were okay and not being attacked by a mob of bloodthirsty Brexiteers. I thought about Grace. She needed her meds. Miss Talland's keys were still on the table. Electric shivers darted down my back. Whatever this was, it must have something to do with Brexit. I needed to get out of there and get into town.

'I'm going,' I said to Sophie.

The clamour of voices and the flicker of phone lights made it hard to focus.

'What do you mean?' she said, her face just inches from mine. 'Going where?'

'I can't stay here,' I said. 'I need to get into town.'

'But you heard what Miss Talland said. We can't leave.'

I pulled the palm of my hand over my head.

'She said we *shouldn't* leave, but it doesn't mean we can't. You in?'

She looked at me, and I knew that I was going alone. I swiped the torch on my phone into life and kissed her on the check. Wide-eyed, she stood perfectly still, receding into darkness as I walked away. I made my way over to the desk and stood with my back touching the edge. Facing the class, my fingers found the irregular metal shapes of the keys behind me. Torch off, I moved towards the door. Sweat, cold and sticky, spread down my back and under my arms. I looked back. There were only panicked shadows, and no sign of Sophie changing her mind. I opened the door and stepped into the ravenous dark of the corridor. It was fully black, the kind of black that makes you see things that aren't there. My heart beat a furious rhythm.

Grace's classroom was beyond the assembly hall, towards the gym, in the new block. Noise from classrooms reverberated around the empty corridor. The space felt bigger, longer, unrecognisable, and I kept as close to the wall as possible. I reached the staff room where raised voices and shouting made me stop. I couldn't identify the first voice I heard.

'... course it was obvious, you xenophobic idiot; all those millions of people, marginalised, what did you expect? That we'd all just have a cappuccino and get over it?'

Then another, lower voice. Mr Grant.

'If this is really happening, then there's no going back for this country. We've been tearing ourselves apart for over three years now. The murder of that politician should have made us realise what we were dealing with.'

'I'd hang them. They're traitors.'

The unfamiliar voice stopped the conversation. Keep moving, I thought. I turned right down the next corridor. Lit only by the weak intermittent light of a ceiling alarm, the corridor was pitch black one second and then a dim, ghostly red the next. I turned on my phone torch. Shadow shapes stretched and twisted in front of me and my tongue ran over desert-dry lips. I was almost at Grace's classroom when a voice boomed behind me. I turned but there was nothing, only distant unidentifiable sounds. My fingers shook as I turned my torch off and tried the nearest door handle. All I could see were ghosts of images. I blinked—nothing. The door opened and I slipped inside. I felt every breath in my chest and my temples throbbed. A muffled voice echoed outside and the crisp *clack* of slow-moving footsteps drew nearer and then passed by. I let out a controlled breath and pressed the home screen on my phone. A weak light allowed me to see something of the room.

'Shit,' I said out loud. I put my hand over my mouth.

It was Mr Andreas, the Headteacher's office. I thought of Stark and my knuckles gave an involuntary throb. He should have been waiting outside. There was a strong smell of burning. Everything was neat and seemed to be in its place except for a small column of smoke rising from one side of the large desk that dominated the room. I crept towards it. The intertwining grey wisps came from a metal wastepaper bin. Why would Mr Andreas be trying to burn anything at a time like this? I thought. And where was he? Without thinking about it, I reached in and pulled out a ball of smouldering, screwed-up paper. I created a space in the middle of the desk and rested my phone against a pile of books so that light spilled across the surface. I checked the door and listened. Nothing. Using both hands, I spread out what remained of the paper, damping down the embers that flared red at the edges. More than half of the A4 sheet was missing. Holding it down with one hand, I brought my phone nearer so I could examine it more closely. On the remaining, blackened section there was an unusual logo near the top right corner. It was a black circle bordering a red, stylised E and a blue U and K arranged vertically to the right of it. I'd seen the logo somewhere before. Immediately below this was an incomplete section of an address. All I could make out was the postcode and HOUSE LIBRARY. I couldn't see who it was addressed to. Beneath the logo it said: *Please destroy this d*

I held the phone light even nearer to the charred paper. I spat on my fingers and rubbed near the top. Letters in a clear, modernist font became visible: NOTES ON EVENTS.

Nothing else was legible. I tried to think, tried to remember. Why did this feel important? An image of the logo flashed into my mind and then was gone. I felt a churning sensation in my stomach, as if the world was spinning faster—out of control.

5. Finding Grace

A distant crash ended my disorientation. I folded up the paper and shoved it in the back pocket of my trousers. I flicked off the light and hurried to the door, opening it a fraction. I looked both ways along the corridor. It was a dark gaping tunnel full of unknown dangers. Voices were coming from somewhere towards the Gym. I left the room and moved towards the commotion, still keeping as near to the walls as possible. Why hadn't the emergency generator come on? Nothing seemed to make sense. Up ahead, darting flashes of light carved the air, not quite reaching the darkness of the ceiling. A shape was coming towards me, running. A girl—younger than me. She didn't see me as she charged past, her eyes bulging and her breath fast like a train. It was like the time Dad took me to the big forest north of the city and we startled a herd of deer. One ran right up to us, only eyeballing us at the last minute. The image stayed with me.

The girl disappeared into the darkness. I walked towards the noise and light and I could pick out individual words, snippets of conversation. Speculation was in the air.

'We didn't vote, so they won't touch us. It's nothing to do with us.'

'Who won't?'

'Them. The people doing this.'

'Yeah, but who are they?'

'It could be Islamic extremists.'

'Or the Russians.'

Someone gave a derisory snort.

'Well, it could.'

'It could also just be a power cut and some nutters on the web having a laugh.'

'Yeah,' came a reassured and almost cheerful response.

I slipped past three year-nine girls huddled near the entrance to the gym, gathered around their mobile phones like Macbeth's witches. They didn't even look at me. Inside, the gym itself was a cauldron of bubbling emotion. Daylight filtered through the floor-to-ceiling windows that faced onto the playing fields, but it felt as if the sun would never properly show its face again. I could sense the barely suppressed hysteria. People were crying in low, pathetic sobs. I touched the arm of a girl I recognised. 'Have you seen...?' She pulled her arm away and just stared at me. Nearer the windows were rows of faces, downcast and unfamiliar. I felt the wild flutters of panic again. Then I saw her. She was sitting alone, head down, on the floor in a corner of the room—in the deep shadow. It was her scarf that caught my eye. Her head appeared to float on a vast black cloud.

'Grace!' I said.

She looked up. Her eyes were red, and she seemed distracted.

'Hey,' she said.

'Are you okay?'

She looked at me for what felt like the longest time and then nodded. The action was too slow, something wasn't right.

'I won't get my meds,' she said. Her head fell forward.

I took her hand. 'Hey, don't worry, it's okay. We're getting out of here.'

She looked up at me again.

'Yeah? But this is a bad thing. It makes me feel...'

Her mouth quivered, and she started to cry. It was all I could do not to cry with her, but there was no time for that.

'Don't, please don't,' I said. 'We'll find Mum, together.'

She shook her head. 'Joel?'

'Yeah?'

'Do you think Mum and Dad are splitting up?'

'What?'

'Getting a divorce, I mean. I think it must be my fault.'

I began about three sentences at once.

'What? No, it's not like that at all. Where did that come from?' I said. 'They argue, yes, but it's just the way old married couples are.'

I tried to smile, but it didn't seem to dent Grace's mindset.

'My illness... it's hard on them, I know.'

'Grace, you've got to snap out of this. They love you; they'd do anything for you. You know that, don't you?'

She looked at me, and it was as if her eyes came back into focus. I wiped a tear from her cheek. Her eyebrows and mouth moved as if to express something that words could not.

'I got a text from Dad and a missed call from Mum,' I said. 'Have you heard anything?'

She shook her head. 'No, nothing.'

'They probably didn't want to worry you.'

'What did Dad say?'

'Well, whether he sent it too soon, or the network has only sent part of it, I don't know, but I only got two words: *I'm sorry.*'

Grace's eyebrows lowered. 'I'm sorry—is that all? Sorry for what?'

I shook my head. 'I don't know. I think they're in the city and trying to tell us something.'

'Like what?'

'That's it, I just don't know.'

Grace covered her face with her hands before slowly removing them. 'I can hear the voice again,' she said.

I crouched down and put my face close to hers. 'Grace. Listen to me. We can't stay here.'

She turned her face away. 'I have to. What's the alternative?'

I shook my head. 'You need your medication. You want to feel better, don't you?'

'Joel, I'm frightened. What's going to happen?'

'I don't know, but they're not letting anyone out of here.'

Her eyes were emerald pools.

'We've got to stick together,' I said.

She nodded. I got to my feet.

'Come on, stand up.'

I offered her my hand. She stood up and straightened her clothes. Students and teachers milled around in the surreal pale blue of the early light. The voice of a male teacher echoed between the hard surfaces, his voice reedy and authoritative.

'Yes, if you could all listen to me, please. Thank you. We have to try and maintain some sort of order...'

I zoned out. People were sitting, standing, not paying attention. They seemed to be waiting for something to happen; waiting for the power to go back on, for things to go back to normal. I knew it more clearly than I'd known anything before. Things were never going back to the way they were.

'Come on, Grace, stay close to me. I've got a car.'

She blinked. 'What?'

'I'll explain on the way. Come on.'

We made our way back towards the main door, sticking close to the walls. We were just about to leave when I felt a hand on my arm.

'Where are you going? Durand, isn't it? You know you have to stay here?'

It was Miss Kimberley from chemistry. I had to think quickly.

'The Head,' I said, trying to maintain eye contact. 'He asked me to see him. I was in a fight, Miss.'

She held my gaze. Sunlight broke through the clouds far behind her. Somewhere in the upper atmosphere, winds were gathering force. She folded her arms.

'I'm not sure he's—'

'I was just in his office, Miss... he sent me to get my sister, Grace.' The lie came easily. I opened my eyes as wide as they would go.

Grace gave me a look.

'She was a witness.'

'Okay,' said Miss Kimberley, rubbing her chin. 'Grace, is this true?'

Grace's eyes flicked to me and then back to her teacher.

'He was in a fight, Miss—with Mitchell Stark.'

Miss Kimberley's mouth dropped at the mention of his name.

'Oh, I see,' she said. 'Alright then, off you go, but you have to come straight back here afterwards. Understood?'

'Yes, Miss.' I said.

She opened the main door and we walked out into the corridor.

'You, girls,' shouted Miss Kimberley, putting her hands on her hips. 'Get back in here immediately. I was very clear that no one was to leave the gym.'

The three witch-girls stood up, eyeballing us as they went meekly back towards the lighted doorway. For a moment, Miss Kimberley stood, silhouetted, before the door closed, plunging us into the fresh echoey darkness of the corridor.

Torches on, we retraced my steps. The door to Mr Andreas' office was still ajar, and inside was lightless and still. We crept past a now-silent staff room. Distant voices, shouts and bangs echoed around us as if we were cast adrift in some giant, stricken ship. We made it to the main entrance without being challenged. The burgeoning day was stuck in twilight, lending a murky, subterranean feel to the all-glass atrium. Being closer to the outside, to trees and birds gave me a momentary lift—a flicker of optimism. Grace pushed the main door. The rush of freezing air that greeted us was a distracting shock.

'Now what?' she said.

I reached into my pocket and pulled out the keys.

'Our *get out of jail, free* card,' I said.

'Whose are those?'

'Never mind, come on.'

Flurries of snow were still falling, but a blizzard looked less likely. Grace wasn't getting her snowman. I shook my head. The car park was full. Crows swarmed in the tall trees that surrounded the perimeter buildings, their rasping calls urgent and unrelenting. Below that, in register, was the distant and reassuring roar of traffic. I couldn't see anyone, but we seemed to be following two sets of footprints.

'Well, which one is it?' said Grace.

'I'm not sure.'

'Press the fob,' she said, her arms wrapped tightly around her.

I pressed the recessed plastic button on the key fob. Nothing. We kept walking, following the footsteps. All the cars were a frosty white. We were nearly at the road that linked to the main road when I saw a small four-door car parked right at the far end. Shrouded in trees, half of it was parked on the kerb. I pressed the fob again. Four orange lights burst into life and the headlights came on.

'Voila,' I said.

The other footprints had gone. I looked around as I wiped a layer of snow off the windscreen.

'You okay to drive?' said Grace.

'Yeah,' I said. Although I'd passed my test first time I wasn't as confident as I sounded.

Grace was already in her seat and examining the contents of the glove compartment. Our breaths clouded in the freezing air, but it was good to be out of the wind, and the intimate, almost claustrophobic interior felt warm by comparison.

'This is a woman's car,' she said, and gave me a long look. 'This is her car: Miss Talland. It is hers, isn't it?'

'It might be,' I said.

'Shit. You're in trouble, Joel.'

'You mean *we're* in trouble.'

Her face fell. I put the keys in the ignition.

'Joel, what's going on. I mean, with everything?'

I looked forward, ready to command the car into life.

'I don't know, but whatever it is, I—'

The back door opened, and someone started to get in. I didn't need to turn around. I knew that perfume.

'Sophie?' I said, my mind not quite able to process what was happening. 'How did you—?'

There was someone else behind her. A hand gripped her arm, pushing her along the seat. Sophie began to cry.

'Joel, I'm sorry, I kind of changed my mind and I was on my way to find you and... he made me tell—'

'Shut up and get in, will ya?'

I looked forward into the rear-view mirror and a broken face filled the view.

6. Interloper

Mitchell Stark.

'You?' I said. Breath punched into frozen air. 'What the hell are you doing here?'

I felt Stark's face just behind my head, his breath hot on my neck. The smell of cheap aftershave and stale cigarettes jolted me back. I could feel the punches and kicks again.

'Shut the fuck up,' he said. 'I know whose car this is, and I've as much right to be here as what you have. You can't treat me like a piece a shit, no more. Not now. I'm going to the rally, and you're taking me.'

Grace screamed and launched herself into the back, arms flailing 'Get out, get out, you fucking racist.'

Stark shrank back, covering his face with his arms. 'Call her off.'

'It's alright Grace,' I shouted. 'It's alright.'

I pulled at her coat. She slowed.

'Just breathe.'

She stopped and retreated, her face wet and flushed.

'You *are* fucking crazy,' said Stark, his hand over his nose.

My fingers tightened around the wheel.

Grace caught her breath, her eyes still wild. 'Don't ever call me that again.' She ran a trembling hand over her hair.

Mine weren't the only eyes taking in the scars on her arm. Line after line, all neatly stacked like an underlined letter.

'What's her fucking problem?' said Stark.

Grace twisted in her seat, the tendons in her neck flexing. I put a hand on her arm and caught her eye. 'Just leave it,' I said. 'Look, Stark, we don't want you here.'

'I'm sorry,' said Sophie, wiping her eyes with her palm.

'Why is *she* here?' said Grace.

'What exactly, like, is your problem?' said Sophie. She started to sob again.

'For fuck's sake, stop blubbing,' said Stark. 'Don't care about your stupid problems. Like I said, Durand—today's the day everything changes. Let's get moving. Come on, come on.'

He thumped the back of my seat. I looked in the rear-view mirror. His face was a mess—puffy with black and blue highlights and patches of dried blood. Grace opened her mouth; I shook my head. She gripped her arm and pushed down into her seat. I turned the key in the ignition and the car burst into life, the blowers coming on full blast. The windows had misted up and for a moment I wondered what would have happened if I'd taken Dad up on his offer to drive him to the city.

'We shouldn't be, like, arguing,' said Sophie. 'I mean, something weird happened back there, with the power and stuff?'

I knew she was right, but the thought of being so close to Stark was intolerable.

'Maybe the people of this country are rising up,' said Grace. 'Fed up with the racists and xenophobes.' Her eyes fixed on somewhere outside the car.

It could have been Dad sitting next to me.

I reversed off the verge, bumping down as we made contact fully with the road.

Stark laughed. 'Yeah, right. The decent, ordinary people of this country.'

'You're scaring me,' said Sophie. 'I think I just want to go home.'

First gear. The car jerked forward, slowed, then jolted forward again.

'You can fucking drive, can't you?' said Stark.

'Of course I can, I'm just not used to this stupid...' I struggled getting second gear, and it crunched into third.

'It's right, here,' said Stark

'Just to be clear,' said Grace. 'My brother was racially abused today by ignorant, moronic thugs...'

Her voice collapsed into rapid breaths and she scratched at her arms with nail-less fingers.

'Grace, don't,' I said.

'We was just standing there, pissing about,' said Stark.

Grace turned around with the speed and venom of a mamba. 'So it's nothing to do with you then? Not your fault?'

Stark squared up. 'Yeah, well, he started it. He shouldn't a hit me.'

'You deserved it,' said Grace.

'Mitchell,' said Sophie. 'Joel didn't start it. You know he didn't. You, like, called him those names and made fun of him.'

Grace turned from Sophie to Stark and put her hand to her mouth. Hearing Stark's first name on Sophie's lips felt like acid in my stomach.

Stark laughed. 'We was having a laugh. It were just banter.'

'Banter?' I snorted. 'Maybe to you.'

We were out of the school and on the open road. Fingers of cold air found their way into the car, undermining the efforts of the heating system.

'Joel,' said Sophie. 'I really do think I want to go home.'

'What do you think this is, a bloody taxi service?' said Grace.

'Grace, cool it,' I said. 'Why are you being like this?'

Sophie dabbed at the corner of her eyes. 'You've never liked me, right from the start.'

Grace breathed in through her nose and out through her mouth. She placed her hands on her lap. 'I guess... I'm a bit stressed and angry right now.'

'Look, Grace,' I said. 'I'll be all right; you'll see.'

Grace put her hands together, as if she were praying. 'I don't want to think about it,' she said, her voice small, fragile.

'Do you lot have to keep droning on about nothing?' said Stark. 'Put the fucking radio on. Get LCB.'

'Why is no one listening to me?' said Sophie. 'If we're, like, all in this together, then we should have an equal say, right?'

'Always used to getting your own way.' said Grace. 'Try thinking of someone else for a change.'

Sophie mimed thumping her ear with the heel of her hand. 'Is it me, or is, like, the same voice saying the same thing, over and over again?'

'Come on,' said Stark. 'Where's that station?'

'I can't, I'm trying to drive.'

'Well, you do it then—you in the front.'

Grace inhaled through her nose, her face, rigid. Words emerged through gritted teeth. 'My name is Grace Durand, and that is the only name I will answer to.'

'I don't care what your fucking name is—change it to LCB.'

He banged his fist down on the back of my seat.

'Just change the goddam channel,' said Sophie. 'Joel was right—you are such a drama queen.'

Shut up, I thought. Grace just sat there. I held my breath. Stark moved within range of the mirror. One of his eyes was closing. The car kangarooed again.

'Grace,' I said. 'Please, change the channel.'

'So, I'm a drama queen, am I?'

I half smiled at her. 'You know you are.'

She glanced at me, and her lips quivered. I wanted to believe it was the flicker of a smile.

'I'll do it for you.' She reached over and scrolled through the stations.

'That's it,' said Stark. He bounced around in his seat.

A man's deep, mature voice filled the car. It sounded safe, reasonable—at first.

... events of the last hour. If you're just tuning in, then you'll know that your power is down, there's no Internet and no phone. Who could be behind this, I hear you ask?

The tone was mocking, sarcastic. It was impossible not to listen.

Well, it's those EU-loving, tree-hugging, climate-change believing lefties. Yes, our very own Remain supporters.

'Holy shit,' said Stark. 'I don't fucking believe it.'

'So the people *are* rising up,' said Grace, her positive tone, unmistakable.

'Oh my god,' said Sophie.

The logo on the burned papers in the head's office burst into my mind. Where had I seen it before? *I love you—whatever happens.* Dad was telling us something. There was an answer just out of reach. I forced myself to concentrate on the iced-up road ahead.

This, ladies and gentlemen, is what, in old-fashioned parlance, is known as a coup d'état. Apologies for using a French expression on a day like today. Not very democratic, is it? While the Government is away—and the Royals too, I might add, it seems the EU pussycats will play. There's been a short statement from a representative of a self-proclaimed 'temporary administration' advising everyone to, and I quote: 'stay calm and do not attempt to travel'. We don't know who these people are yet, or whether the military are going along with this travesty. What we at LCB say, and by the way, we will continue broadcasting throughout this crisis, is that there is only one way that we, the decent, law-abiding people of Britain need to deal with this. We need to take to the streets.

Stark was loving it—fidgeting, rubbing his hands and nodding like some demented pigeon.

If these traitors do have the army behind them, well, then we've got a real fight on our hands. But we will never surrender. This country will be great again. Get out there and fight.

'Yes. Fucking yes!' shouted Stark, punching the air. 'They are so dead. You hear me? We'll sort out you Remain cunts once and for all.'

There was nothing to say. It was like being in a cage with an alien species as he raged, spitting his bile into the back of my neck. We sat quietly and let him rant, as the wintry world flashed by outside like some warped dream. I thought about how this might end and I shuddered, every fibre of my body gripped by an icy dread.

7. Trapped

Dad always told me how to deal with confrontation. *Joel*, he'd say, *look the other way, count to ten—anything, just don't act on that first rush of emotion. Think.* Well, I'd given it a lot of thought. I wanted to turn around, crush Stark's face into a pulp and kick his lifeless body down the road. Just imagining it made me feel better for a second or two. I couldn't think about Dad any more. Outside, the snow was coming down heavily and it was hard to see ahead. The steady roar of the blowers dominated. Sophie was quiet, apart from an occasional sob. Her face was bathed in the flickering blue light from her phone. Grace's fingers gripped the fabric of her jacket, pulling it into tight ridges. I could feel Stark moving around in the seat behind me.

'What's the holdup?' he said, lowering his head, trying to see out of each window.

I fiddled with the control stick and the wipers moved big wedges of fluffy crystals to either side of the windscreen. We were still some distance from the roundabout on the ring road, yet the traffic was slowing. There were blue flashing lights ahead.

'There's some problem,' I said. 'I think they're stopping cars.'

'No cops,' said Stark. 'I'm going to the city.'

'We're all going to the city,' said Grace.

Sophie said something under her breath. I could see uniformed figures, dark against the snow. The sick feeling in my stomach lifted for a moment.

'What's that noise?' said Sophie.

'Sounds like the engine,' I said.

'Shut up,' said Stark, tilting his head to one side.

It was a deep roar, coming from all around the car. A wave of sound hit us and seemed to reach into the middle of my body, rearranging my insides. I braked and we skidded to a stop. I looked up and caught a black shape moving low and at great speed across the sky.

'Shit,' said Stark. 'It's a—'

Another hammer blow of sound hit the car. We all ducked down and waited. A second shape shot across my field of vision. It was going too fast to register any detail.

'Plane,' said Grace, sitting up straight in her seat.

'That was low,' I said.

'I don't like it,' said Sophie.

Stark was glued to the back window, trying to follow the progress of the jets. There was only a dull, generalised rumble, like distant thunder.

'Our boys are coming to sort things out,' said Stark.

He didn't sound entirely convinced.

'You have all the answers, don't you?' said Grace.

'What were that?' said Stark.

'Nothing,' she said, looking forward the whole time.

'Yeah, well...' said Stark. 'You'll soon get the only answer you understand.'

I wound my window down to get a better view of the other cars in front, which had come to a near standstill. The air was biting and snowflakes settled then melted on my skin. Stretching some way ahead was a long line of red tail lights.

'Shut the fucking window,' said Stark.

I wound the window up. He leaned forward.

'Pull out, go round them.'

'What?' I said. 'But there are police there, we can't.'

'Yeah, we can. Do it.'

Grace touched my arm. 'They might stop all cars getting through.' She nodded.

Walls were rising all around me, and there was only one way out. I looked in the rear-view mirror; exhaust clouds almost obscured the queue of cars behind. My heart pounded and every hair follicle on my body came alive.

'Come on,' said Stark.

'Just go for it,' said Grace.

'I don't think we should,' said Sophie.

I thought of Dad and Mum and the dinner planned for this evening. Just the four of us. A storm was rising inside me. *I love you.* There was something I was missing. I slammed the car into reverse, and we jolted backwards, hitting the car behind us. Sophie's hand muffled a shout. There was a ringing in my ears.

Lights flashed, and a car horn sounded. A shape emerged from the car behind and moved towards us.

'Move it,' said Stark, his voice an animal cry. I steeled my jaw and pushed the gearstick into first. The car shot forward, sliding wildly as we left the line of traffic and headed towards the blue flashing lights.

'Come on,' he shouted as we gained speed.

Air seethed through clamped teeth and my throat gathered raw sounds. Grace pressed herself back into her seat and shook her head. 'This isn't good, this isn't good.'

Sophie's voice was building towards a continuous scream.

'Keep going, keep going,' bellowed Stark.

I could feel his excitement, and for a moment I was part of it.

'Slow down,' said Grace.

'I can't.'

Two patrol cars blocked the road, but there was a way through to the side—over a snowy embankment. The officer held up a gloved hand. I put my foot down on the accelerator.

'Oh my god,' cried Sophie.

'Joel, you're going to hit him,' shouted Grace.

Car horns blared. At the last minute I swerved and the car bounced over the embankment. The cop ducked down and shouted into a walkie-talkie. Stark whooped with delight and there was a popping sound, like fireworks, from behind us. A dull thud came from somewhere at the back of the car.

'What was that?' said Sophie, her voice one notch down from hysterical.

I had too much adrenaline coursing through my veins to care. My chest was heaving, and beads of sweat burst on my forehead. Grace was bent forward with her hands over the back of her head.

'Wooh,' hollered Stark, jumping up and down in his seat.

We flashed past a line of headlights facing us, strung out like stars in the snowy gloom.

Stark's hand squeezed my neck. It was cold and rough.

'You fucking did it, Durand. Nice one. I always took you for a pussy but that were dope.'

Grace leaned forward, her face hidden by both hands. She was shaking.

'They, like, shot at us, didn't they?' said Sophie.

I stared ahead. I didn't want her to be right.

'This is a fucking war,' said Stark.

I didn't really know what fear was, but I was sure it was there with us in the car—it felt dark and cold with sharp teeth, and I could hear it in Stark's voice.

The line of cars thinned, and we entered the dark, power-deprived outer suburbs of the city. I put both hands on the steering wheel and looked at Grace as I spoke. She was biting what was left of the skin around her nails.

'They're blocking off the city,' I said, forcing the words out.

'Turn the bloody heating up,' said Stark. 'It's fucking freezing.'

It was getting colder and the cotton wool sky seemed to have closed in again. I reached for the blower settings. Grace turned her head away from me.

'I hope they're alright,' she said. 'Mum and Dad.'

'She'll be there,' I said. 'It's going to be okay.'

'Hey, stop whispering,' said Stark. 'Turn the radio back up.'

Grace reached for the volume before I had a chance to react.

'That's better,' said Stark.

... just coming in that there is fierce fighting in parts of the capital. There are unconfirmed reports of looting and that several major buildings are burning out of control. There has still been no official group claiming responsibility for this morning's attempted coup, but the military are definitely involved, at least some sections are...

'Told you there'd be a fight back,' said Stark, a grin widening across his face. 'Just need to get to town. The lads will sort you lot out.'

I wanted to say something but stopped myself. It felt as if we'd climbed to the top of a rollercoaster and we were about to begin our descent. Grace's hands were fists.

'It's the do-gooding Remainers what's got everyone so riled,' said Stark. 'All we needed were to get Brexit done, kick the fucking migrants out and get back sovereignty.'

'Really?' said Grace. 'You actually believe all that propaganda crap?'

'Grace, don't,' I said.

'It's not fucking proper... whatever,' said Stark. 'My dad says this country started going downhill after the war. Should never a let you lot in—taking us jobs, claiming benefits and getting houses.'

'You lot?' said Grace. 'Listen to yourself. I'm as British as you are.'

'Don't make me laugh. Look at you.'

Something snapped in my head. I jerked the steering wheel to the left and swerved off the road, scraping along a metal barrier. Sophie and Grace screamed. I felt Stark's fingers on my shoulder and stamped on the brakes as hard as I could. We skidded and came to a dead stop with the engine racing. We were all thrown forward, but only so far. Stark hit the back of my headrest——hard.

My breath was fast in my throat. 'Don't you ever talk to her like that again, you hear me?'

Stark groaned. He lay back in his seat, holding his head. I jumped out into freezing wind and snow, ripped open his door and grabbed his arm. In one move I pulled him bodily out and onto the snow. In his black trousers and bloodstained shirt he looked a miserable sight. My chest heaved and every muscle was ready.

'Get up,' I shouted. 'Come on. Get up.'

He looked up at me with narrowed eyes. I felt a strong grip on my arms, holding me back.

'Joel, don't.'

I turned and Grace's face was in front of mine. Shrouded in snow, she shook her head. 'This isn't you,' she said. She put her hand on my chest.

The world lost its red haze, and I saw the green in her eyes. We were on the edge of a dual carriageway. Cars, their headlights blazing, swished anonymously through the snow. Sophie walked around the car, holding her phone up in front of her.

'Are you filming?' I said.

She stopped. 'Yeah, it's kind of for later.'

'Later?' I said.

'You know, when 4G's back on.'

The information punched deep into my brain. Connections. Conclusions.

'That is so not cool,' I said.

Clouds of white vapour spewed from the exhaust into the snowy gloom. Sophie lowered the phone. 'I didn't think...'

Stark laughed, sat up and put the back of his hand to his nose. His eyes burned. 'Don't let him fucking push you around, blondie. I want evidence.' Blood was vivid as he pulled his hand away.

'Stop calling me that,' she said.

I wanted to hurt Stark, to make him accountable for his words. Grace moved between us and stood over him like some colossus. She stared down at his lowly form, needing no words to convey her disgust. He tried to stand up. His face was a mess. I took a deep breath and stepped towards the driver's door.

'We're not just going to leave him here?' said Sophie. She pulled her hand through her hair, the wet straggly ends beginning to darken and clump.

A dark, anger-fuelled voice in my head told me to leave him, to get in the car and drive.

'Joel, he'll freeze.'

'Hey, I'm not a fucking parcel,' said Stark. He stood up. On his feet, he was more a cold, twisted scarecrow than a Brexit-loving thug. His stained shirt stuck to his body, and shivers convulsed his frame.

I looked at Grace, and I could see Mum in her profile. In the rush of wind and energy, I heard her voice. It was a small voice, but one I couldn't ignore. I shook my head. 'You're right, we can't live by his rules.'

Stark laughed.

'One more word...' I said.

My numbed fingers balled into tight fists. Snow whipped at my cheeks and my eyes gripped and held him. 'Get in.'

Stark put a hand on the roof of the car. For a moment I didn't know whether he was going to stay or run. His eyes flashed a hungry desperation. He moved towards the back.

'No, in the front,' I said.

He brushed snow off one side of his body. Doors slammed. We were back in our intimate bubble. Stark muttered and fidgeted. Melting snow ran down the back of my neck.

'Let's just try and get through this,' I said.

Sophie's eyes were aqueous diamonds in the rear-view mirror. The headlights traced two brilliant tunnels of light through falling snow. The tyres spun at first, but then we moved forward. Through the churning windscreen wipers, the sky was grey and heavy. Was this the bright, clear future the politicians promised?

I turned back onto the road and rejoined the small number of cars heading towards the city. On the other side of the central barrier, cars were bumper to bumper. We followed compressed car tracks and reached the approach to the motorway bridge. We crawled across. Beneath us in the wintry gloom, every lane in both directions was jammed with stationary cars. Exhaust fumes swirled as low cloud and black shapes moved in disorderly lines on the hard shoulder.

'They're walking,' said Grace. 'All of them.'

'Yeah,' I said.

'Everything's falling apart.'

'Well, we know whose fault that is, don't we?' said Stark.

'Don't push it,' I said.

Stark squirmed in his seat and wrapped his arms around himself. Beyond the bridge were industrial units with whitened frontages bordered by wide, empty pavements. Bare trees formed snowy sentinels above queuing cars. The sun didn't seem able to establish a hold on the day.

'Brexit has, like, screwed everything,' said Sophie.

The engine throbbed and the blowers spewed out lukewarm air.

'I thought we weren't discussing that?' said Grace, looking at me.

We moved forward again, slowly at first and then gathered momentum. I didn't want to get drawn into another pointless discussion about Brexit. Something bad was going on and we were dealing with it as best we could. Grace folded her arms and sat back in her seat. Stark cleared his throat. When he spoke, he sounded like a robot on antidepressants.

'Dad said we should make a new border just south of Coventry. Stick Remainers in the south and keep the north for ourselves.'

I shifted in my seat. Just like India and partition, I thought.

'Daddy would like that,' said Sophie. 'He and mummy both voted Leave.'

For a brief, frightening moment I saw a future world divided into media-controlled fiefdoms, where supplicant populations lived in permanent fear and suspicion of their neighbours. Anything seemed possible now that we were living through a dystopian version of our future lives.

'Yeah, but what do *you* think?' said Grace.

'You what?' said Stark.

'You keep saying what your dad thinks.'

Stark's hands moved over and around each other and he squeezed the ends of each finger. 'Yeah, well—he's right, isn't he? You fucking come over here, swamping this country.'

'I'm still not hearing it,' said Grace.

Stark thumped the frame of the door. 'Just get off my fucking back, will you?

We're swamped, that's all... swamped.'

Grace retreated into the shadows. We arrived at a big intersection where the snow was pricked with darkened traffic lights and street furniture. It looked like a Christmas scene gone wrong.

'What's that smell?' said Sophie.

Ahead of us, several cars had collided. Smoke poured from the open doors of one, while another had settled almost on its side. People and cars negotiated the smash. The smell grew stronger.

'Keep going,' said Grace.

I heard the ping of Sophie's camera and tutted.

'This is scary,' she said.

There were people on the roadside, walking away from the city. Two women came close to the car, the older limping and leaning on the other. She waved and shouted.

'What's she saying?' said Sophie.

Stark replied, his voice lacking its usual swagger.

'Go back.'

8. Freethinking Woman

There was nothing to say. We seemed outside time—forced together in a snowy cocoon. We could hear each other's breath, smell each other's smell and our faces seem unable to disguise our inner thoughts. It was like a terrible excitement.

'We're going to make it, aren't we?' said Grace.

'Don't worry. We've got time,' I said. 'We'll make it.'

It was a struggle to see signs and directions. Snow completely obscured metal hoardings. The car slid, and the engine made sudden variations in sound as the wheels spun and lost traction.

'What's the rush?' said Sophie. The blue light from her phone clicked off.

'None of your business,' said Grace.

'I was just asking.'

Silence.

'But it must be something, you know, like, important?'

I shifted in my seat, and the car wobbled.

'Look, if you must know, Grace has run out of her meds,' I said.

Grace leaned forward, both hands pressed down on the tops of the front seats. 'That's private, Joel. You had no right.'

'I know. I'm sorry,' I said. 'And in an ideal world where all this wasn't going on I wouldn't say anything, but it's vital that you get those drugs.'

'What drugs?' said Sophie.

'Look, I'm fine, absolutely fine,' said Grace. 'It's not like I'm...'

'Crazy?' said Stark.

I took my foot off the accelerator. 'I'm warning you, Stark. One more comment like that and I swear...'

'Why are you always such a dick, Mitchell?' said Sophie.

'Did you hear me?' I said.

Stark smirked. 'Lighten up, bro. It's just banter.'

I couldn't see Grace's face properly in the mirror, but I knew that I'd upset her. 'Grace, I'm sorry. I'm just trying to help.'

'I'm not crazy,' she said.

Stark opened his mouth as if to say something but closed it again. He looked towards me and then glanced round at Grace. There was something in his expression that I hadn't seen before. It was as if, just for a moment, he'd let his guard down.

'So, what is wrong with you?' said Stark.

'Just shut it, Stark,' I said.

'No,' said Grace. 'No one ever asks me questions like that, they just either ignore me or treat me like I'm some kind of freak.'

'But, you're not. Are you?' said Stark.

Grace pulled the face that Mum used so often, of mild irritation—lips pressed together and pushed to one side.

'No, I'm not.'

'So?'

'I hear voices.'

'Seriously?'

No one said anything. The deep thrum of the engine filled the tight space. Outside was white, total white. Grace cleared her throat and her fingers played around her cheek.

'It's a woman's voice. Sometimes she says amazing things and I feel powerful and strong. Then there are the other times...'

I'd never heard her talk like this before. She'd told me something of how she felt, but seeing her face in the mirror, she looked different, like she was in some sort of trance. Her eyes were wide and her voice was low and soft.

'She's cruel. She says I'm useless; ugly; pathetic. I feel as if I want to crawl into a hole and die. It went on for years until Mum made me get help.'

'That sounds really crappy,' said Sophie.

Grace lifted her chin. 'I have psychosis. It's controlled by drugs.'

'So, you can see why we've got to get to the city,' I said. 'We're meeting Mum. She picked the meds up this morning.'

Grace put the knuckle of her hooked finger into her mouth and bit it.

Stark turned around. 'This woman. Is she, you know—is she talking to you now?'

Grace nodded and lowered her head.

'It's nothing bad, is it?' I said.

'Yep. The world's gonna end and it's all my fault.'

'Fuck,' said Stark.

'That must be, like, so frightening,' said Sophie.

'I don't want your pity,' flashed Grace.

'I didn't mean...'

My earlier assessment of Grace as a big-haired, freethinking woman wasn't quite accurate. For the first time I had a real sense of what she was going through.

Stark ran nail-bitten fingers over his chin and inclined his head towards the back. 'I didn't mean them things, you know, that I...'

From the shadows, Grace's voice was deep and soft. 'I know.'

I felt a wave of love and admiration for my complicated sister. For a time, no one spoke and the car seemed filled with thoughts and unspoken words.

'I was just thinking,' said Sophie. 'What if... well, what if, like, everything doesn't go back to the way it was?'

The question hung in the air.

'I mean, I want to get a qualification,' she said. Her voice sounded different and I could hear an unexpected yearning and sensitivity.

I turned my head a fraction, trying to catch her eyes in the mirror.

'No one takes me seriously. You were right, Grace; I'm, like, just an Instagram airhead to everyone.'

Grace's head rested against the window. She didn't move. I could feel words forming in my mouth but something stopped me from saying them.

'I miss my room,' said Grace. 'It's kind of safe, and I can put music on and for a while, she goes away.'

Stark moved from one side of his seat to the other. He touched his eye, which was almost closed, and a sickly shade of green.

'I miss, Archie.'

I turned the blower down one notch. The corners of Stark's mouth curled down.

'Archie?' said Sophie.

'Me dog.'

'Oh.'

I cleared my throat. 'I want to travel—see the world, before University.'

'He's won awards for agility.'

'Daddy said I can be anything I want to be.'

Grace sat forward. 'Stop it, stop it.' There was a cry in her voice. 'We're fooling ourselves. We can't go back. This is real and I'm frightened.'

'I know,' I said. 'But we have to be positive.'

'I'm frightened too,' said Sophie.

'There was something,' I said. 'I wasn't going to mention it, but...'

'What?' said Grace.

'When I was coming to get you, I found something in Mr Andreas' office. I think—'

'He were in on it,' said Stark, almost to himself. He looked as if he'd solved the problem of nuclear fusion.

I shook my head. 'Who was in on what?'

'Andreas.'

To our left, lights flickered in the windows of a pub. A line of dirty brown earth led up to its front door. Stark touched somewhere on his forehead, just above his eyes, and slowly traced a figure eight with his fingers.

'Like, our, Mr Andreas?' said Sophie.

He carried on as if she hadn't spoken.

'I waited outside, like I were told to do and I heard him.'

We slowed at a junction, allowing other cars to pass.

'I were still outside when the power went out,' he said. 'Andreas come out, and he were all panicky, and boy was he in a fucking hurry to get out a there. Fucking weird, it were. His phone were working, and he kept saying somethin' about notes on events.'

My head spun towards him. I could see the charred paper, smell the remains of the botched attempt to destroy it. I waited for the next bit of information. I changed down, forcing our way through the murky-grey slush. We were on the outer ring road that would eventually take us to the city.

'He knew it were going to happen,' said Stark. 'He said it were brought forward by a day and that he'd meet 'em in the usual place in the city. I never liked how he looked at me. Couldn't tell whether he wanted to expel me or fuck me.'

I didn't want to know if he was being serious.

'That's gross, Mitchell,' said Sophie.

'Why would he be interested in you?' said Grace.

'I'm a bit of rough,' he said. 'Older guys like that.'

I saw a brief window into Stark's world. It seemed a dark and squalid place.

'Eugh,' said Sophie.

I needed to think. My head felt as if it was stuffed with information but with no conclusions. I decided not to mention what I'd found.

An unbroken outline of factories, storage facilities and garages lay between us and the thick, grey-white of the sky. Deserted buildings looked reborn in their ice-crystal blankets. We took a right, following signs for the city.

'It's stopped snowing,' said Sophie.

She was right. I turned the wipers off.

'Can we listen to the radio again,' said Grace. 'Maybe a channel with some proper news.'

Stark muttered something under his breath.

'Yeah, okay,' I said.

The housing stock changed again. Detached and semi-detached properties with neat gardens sported white overcoats. I turned up the volume on the radio and tried the other presets. The fourth button yielded a man's well-spoken and rounded voice. He was interviewing a younger woman.

'*... legal precedents for an intervention of this kind?*' said the male voice.

'*No, I'm afraid not, Jeremy. The law is clear. A coup, or an overthrow, is an illegal and overt seizure of a state by the military or other elites within the state apparatus. But I imagine the group behind today's action will no doubt consider themselves defenders of democracy.*'

'*But they're traitors, aren't they?*'

'*That's a strong word to use.*'

'*Yes, it is. But that's the legal definition of someone who illegally attempts to overthrow the State, isn't it?*'

Houses and rows of ancient oak trees passed by in a frozen blur as the conversation unfolded. Sophie leaned forward.

'*Technically, yes,*' said the woman, sounding a little irritated, as if she didn't enjoy being directed in this way. '*But there are insurgent groups and freedom fighters throughout history that have reflected the democratic will of the people.*'

'*Yes, but—*'

'*Egypt, for instance. The so-called Arab Spring. It was an uprising—a coup by any other name.*'

'I like this woman,' said Grace. 'She's not letting him browbeat her.'

'Surely, you can't compare a country from the middle east with an established democracy like ours?'

There was silence for a moment and then the woman spoke again.

'You mean our class-ridden, post-Imperialist, democracy?'

The interviewer gave a derisory I-know-better-than-you, laugh.

'Now you're sounding like—'

'Like what? Like the person who murdered an elected British politician on the streets of this enlightened nation?'

'Well, I... ' The interviewer stumbled.

'My mother has a great expression' said the woman interviewee: *'Someone makes the balls, but gets someone else to throw them.'* The man tried to interrupt, but she pressed on. *'What I mean by that, is that over the last three years, certain figures in the political arena, and we all know who they are, have used their platform to infer, to suggest, to imply that the problems that this country faces are due to foreigners coming to stay and work. Their rhetoric has allowed the racists and xenophobes the freedom to assert themselves. They are emboldened.'*

'Miss Turner, you are moving away from the central issue with these wild—'

'Am I? I think this is fundamental to the argument and why there has been this uprising, today. The real coup happened in 2016 when the State was effectively the victim of a right-wing takeover. How else could the lies and propaganda that followed be tolerated?'

'I will have to ask you—'

'Go on, tell him,' shouted Grace. She leaned forward and held her clenched fist just below her chin. Stark was making low mumbling sounds.

'To keep quiet about this? I think too much of the negativity and downright lies that have been expressed during the last three years have gone unchallenged. August broadcasters like yourselves have, too often, provided a platform for racist ideology.'

The man spoke, and this time did not hide his disapproval.

'You were invited on this programme to provide a particular perspective on this current crisis, instead—'

'Notes on Events.'

'I'm sorry—what?'

There was a bass noise and a scraping sound, as if someone were fumbling with the cover of the microphone. The man cleared his throat, and a tinny disembodied voice barked an instruction.

'Listeners, I'm sorry, but Miss Turner appears to have ended this interview rather, er, prematurely. Her robust views will no doubt stimulate a great deal of discussion. Given the unusual events, we will, in a few minutes, be going over to the newsroom for a news briefing.'

A bland piece of orchestral music played.

'She was incredible,' said Grace. 'I've never heard anyone talk like that before.'

'My dad should listen to her,' said Sophie. 'He just wants to turn the clock back.'

'It's all bollocks,' said Stark. 'You lot have no fucking idea what's happening on the street.'

'Of course we do, we just don't agree with it,' said Grace.

A series of bumps lifted us from our seats.

'Don't you fucking get it?' said Stark. 'The people have decided. They know who's to blame for no jobs and no future. They want their country back, the way it were. Pure and simple. Close the borders—no more immigration.'

'Didn't you hear a word the woman on the radio said?' I looked to the road, to Stark and back again.

'We had a referendum, and we won, fair and square,' said Stark.

We all started talking at once.

'Well we did, didn't we?' he said, his voice restored to its cocky swagger.

'I suppose so,' said Sophie.

Stark laughed. 'Suppose so? It were the will of the people.'

'It was—then,' I said. 'But things have changed.'

'*We* couldn't vote, then,' said Grace.

'And people change their minds,' I said.

Our bubble was well and truly ruptured. Stark's dog, Sophie's plans and Grace's room seemed a million years' ago.

'I can hear bees,' said Sophie.

'You what?' I said.

'Bees...'

There it was. Above the sound of the engine, an insect-like buzz rose, but with something lower, more menacing.

'Fuck me, it's the Angels,' said Stark, his voice breathy with uncontained excitement. He turned around, craning his neck to see out of the back window.

'Angels?' said Grace.

'Hell's Angels,' said Stark, with a note of triumphalism.

'Bikes,' I said. 'And by the sounds of it, lots of them.'

A deep throbbing bass rattled our bones. I could see something in the mirror, a black enveloping cloud ready to smother us.

'There's fucking hundreds of them,' said Stark.

'Joel, should we get off the road?' said Grace.

I shook my head. 'I think we should just keep going and not do anything to attract their attention.'

They buzzed around us like big fat metal flies. Grace's hand went to her chest and she shrank back in her seat. I tried to keep looking ahead, but I felt a dark energy filling up the spaces between us. Stark jumped around in his seat shaking his fist, like a kid on his birthday.

'They're, like, going to the rally, aren't they?' said Sophie.

'Course they are,' said Stark. 'That's it, now. Game over.'

The riders seemed impervious to the snow as their insect heads reflected our eyes back at us. They swarmed past, a dark mass of leather and shiny metal, belching fumes until each was swallowed up into snow and ice. I thought about Mum and Dad. Would they meet these intimidating figures? I felt cold all over at the thought of it. We had to get to the city. If we could meet Mum, then we could find Dad. It was a plan—something to cling on to.

'There's, like, a funny smell,' said Sophie.

Grace screwed up her face. 'It smells like... oh, god.'

It was a bad smell—a really bad smell. We were in treeless streets lined with once-grand tenements and houses. Even with the simplification of the snow, they loomed stern and forbidding. Behind them, low-rise flats sat squat and unkempt. A thick column of dark smoke lit by blue strobing light rose a short distance away. A solitary car passed us in the opposite direction.

'It looks rough here,' I said.

Ahead of us, a car was on its side, wisps of smoke rising from its burned out husk.

Stark sat up in his seat. His eyes narrowed.

'This is where *I* live.'

9. War

I'd never been to this part of the city before and its oppressive, menacing sprawl made me want to floor it and get out of there. If I'd grown up here, how would I have turned out? I wondered. Stark scanned the road as we made our way around the wreck of the car and through banks of grey slush. We passed a shop with smashed windows, its entrance door wide open.

'They're here,' said Stark.

'Who are?' I said.

'The residents.'

Flurries of snow blew around tight corners and shadows stirred in the in-between spaces. It felt as if we were the only people alive on the planet.

'Maybe we shouldn't have come this way,' said Sophie. Her hand tightened around the top of my seat.

'You say you live here?' said Grace.

The wind had picked up, and it howled around the car like an impatient ghoul. Stark pointed beyond the immediate structures to a tower block, its exterior clad in pale blues and whites.

'Tenth floor. Lift's broke, water's dodgy and the cladding's fucked.'

Sophie gasped and sat up. 'Who are *they*?'

The figures came out of nowhere—nine of them, all in dark clothes, moving from the edges of the buildings into the middle of the road. They walked slowly and deliberately with what looked like baseball bats and machetes swinging low from icicle hands. Spread over the whole of the road, they stopped. Beyond them, the road seemed to narrow.

'Turn round, turn round,' said Sophie, on stifled high-anxiety breaths. 'I knew we shouldn't have come this way.'

I stopped the car and looked down to find reverse. I pushed the gear stick and a terrible grating sound filled the car.

'Come, on,' I said.

'They're coming this way,' said Grace.

'Come on, Joel, hurry up,' said Sophie.

A single figure, ahead of the others, moved through the snow like a wraith.

'Oh shit,' said Stark.

'What?' I said.

His hand went to the eyebrow above his bad eye. 'I thought he were inside.' He swallowed, and his tongue played over his thin top lip.

It was the red baseball cap that first caught my eye. Matching trainers, their laces hanging loose, bulged below shiny sports trousers. Hands thrust deep into the pockets of a blue hoodie and a cigarette jutted from pursed lips.

'Don't say nothing,' said Stark. 'He's a fucking nutcase.'

Stark wound down his window and leaned out. Cold air poured into the car and our breaths ballooned in front of us. Stark was smiling, smiling as if he couldn't stop. It changed his face completely.

'Hey, Kyle,'

The figure walked towards the open window. He took the cigarette from his mouth and blew out a cloud of smoke. He flicked the stub with his middle finger, and it spun into oblivion. I took my hand off the gearstick. The engine idled. The youth called Kyle looked about twenty, with a tattoo of a snake running from above his right eye down to his neck. He leaned in and his lips peeled back into something resembling a smile but could just as easily have been a snarl.

'Hey, Starky. It's you, man,' he said, his voice a thin, mean drawl. The pair did an elaborate knuckle and finger handshake. 'What's with the face?'

Melting water from Kyle's cap ran down his nose and dripped onto Miss Talland's upholstery. A film of sweat glistened on the back of Stark's neck. Some emotion was working on his smile, pulling at the corners of his mouth—undoing it.

'This?' said Stark, pointing to his eye as if he hadn't noticed it before. 'Just sorting out business, man, you know.' His body language screamed nonchalance but was fooling no one. He looked a mess.

'And what the fuck are you wearing? School's out, I guess.'

'Yeah, it's sick,' said Stark. 'What a fucking crazy day. You coming into town?'

'Course... we're chasing down those cunts.'

Kyle came a little closer, leaned in and inspected us. He looked like a weasel minus the intellect. I could feel my bowels loosen under his scrutiny.

'Who are these losers?'

This is it, I thought. They'll kill us. I clasped my hands together to stop them from shaking.

'Them?' said Stark. 'They're cool.'

I could hear Grace's tremulous intake of breath behind me. My skin was alive with electrical activity. I commanded my lips to keep still, to keep my face, expressionless. The bony stick insect nodded and leaned in just a fraction more. I could smell something like sour milk. For a moment, he opened his eyes, and I felt their cold, watery-blue emptiness. They flashed at Sophie.

'Get out.'

The air froze. I felt sick. Kyle stepped back and away from the car.

'No,' said Sophie, from behind her hand.

Stark's head didn't move, but every other muscle flexed. 'Hey, Kyle, man, come on...'

'You heard me.'

Stark turned his head towards us. He whispered through his rictus smile. 'Play along. Don't do nothing stupid.'

I felt as if I should say something gallant, something suited to my gender, like: *it'll be alright,* or: *don't worry, I'll protect you*; but every thought, every idea felt hollow and meaningless. This was the end of the road.

We got out of the car like dutiful robots. I knew it must be cold, but I felt nothing. The hungry wind devoured Sophie's dull sobs. Grace kept her chin up and projected an air of grim resignation. Stark wouldn't stop talking. This particular robot was malfunctioning, with arms that had a life of their own.

'Kyle, mate. I got to get to that rally. Got my people waitin.'

The information had no effect. Kyle wasn't listening. He was too busy scrutinizing us. We huddled together behind Stark—the vanguard of our resistance. I knew if I tried to run, my legs wouldn't work. It was all I could do to stay upright.

'Nice hair, sister,' he said to Grace.

She looked straight ahead. Kyle didn't seem to notice the twitch in the corner of her eye. He walked round and gestured to Sophie with his finger.

'You.'

She didn't move.

'Joel?' she said, her voice cracking.

Kyle took a step towards her and in response to some primal reflex, my legs moved and I was standing between them. He was shorter than me. I pulled cold air into my lungs and the pins and needles in my arms and legs subsided a little. He moved closer, and I felt his breath, sour in my nostrils.

'Get out of my way,' he said.

Words bubbled in my mind, but my throat was too tight for communication. I shook my head. The wind howled around us and flurries of white crystals danced in complicated spirals. From the corner of my eye I saw Stark move towards us. I felt Sophie's hands grab the back of my jacket. Grace opened her mouth. Don't say anything, I thought.

Stark play-punched Kyle's arm. 'Hey, Kyle, mate. You want some blow?'

Kyle's eyes were conjuring demons, and the fires of hell, but I stared back. Dad always said you had to stand up to bullies. I could feel a pricking at the corners of my eyes.

'What?' said Kyle, his eyes locked to mine.

'It's the best—here.'

Stark pulled out a small bag from his trouser pocket. It had what looked like a small amount of flour at the bottom. Kyle broke his stare and from between full lips, small yellow teeth appeared.

'Nice.'

'The real deal.'

Stark held out the bag, and Kyle took a step away from me. Sophie, still gripping the back of my jacket, breathed out in quick controlled sobs. Grace's hand went to her mouth. Kyle held up the bag. Sounds of approval from the other gang members spiked across the icy street. They moved towards us. Kyle snorted some of the powder from the hollow next to his thumb. He rubbed his finger over his gums. I put my arms around Sophie. She was shaking all over.

'It's good,' said Kyle. 'You want something for this?'

The answer was implicit in the question. Stark got the message.

'On the house, bro.'

Kyle nodded, but the slow tilt of his head seemed more like a mocking sneer. He took a step back towards me. 'This boy's got a fucking problem.'

One side of Kyle's face jerked, and his eyes narrowed, finding mine. A heat flowed through me. My muscles tensed. I was a nice boy from the nice part of town on an ordinary school day, but my blood was up and things were different now. I didn't dare speak, but my lips twitched and my chest rose and fell, breath heavy through my nose. He moved like a fox, his face directly in front of mine.

'No one fucking crosses me.'

I saw his hand move as a vague shape and then felt a pressure on my stomach. It was like a soft punch—as if I'd swallowed ice. A thin coldness spread towards my back. Kyle turned and walked away, holding the bag high. He wiped something on his trousers. There was a sound in my ears. I turned my head, and Grace's mouth was open. I knew she was screaming, but there was only a high-pitched ringing sound. My legs—how was I standing when there was no feeling? I put a leg back to steady myself, and felt Sophie's hand in the small of my back. Then the pain hit, and the world rushed back in with it.

'Joel?' said Sophie. 'Are you—?'

'He's stabbed him,' said Grace. 'Oh my god.'

Snow swirled in a vortex around me. It was hard to tell up from down and I felt impossibly cold. I made myself look down at my waist. Both hands were tight against my stomach. I prised them away and let the image fill my mind. I'd seen the sequence a hundred times in movies, but there came the sickening realisation that this was happening to me. The palms of my hands were covered in blood. My blood. He'd stabbed me. I looked around with questioning eyes, unable to form suitable words. I must have looked like an oxygen-starved goldfish.

'Now get the fuck off my patch.'

Kyle's voice was soaked up by the elements as he turned towards the others.

They gathered in a tight semicircle, oblivious to us. Stark motioned with his head for us to get back in the car. The engine was still running. I felt hands pull me and jolts of unbelievable pain as they bundled me into the passenger seat. Grace sat in beside me. A wave of nausea made me close my eyes and my head fell back on the headrest. Doors slammed, and I heard everyone's voices at the same time. I seemed to be floating. Grace's voice punched above the others.

'Of course I can drive—I've had a lesson.'

A sudden pressure pushed me back in my seat. I opened my eyes a fraction. The snowy tops of buildings and trees moved past in a blur.

'Fuck,' said Stark. 'Why the hell did he do that?'

Sophie's voice was high and excited. 'He needs a doctor.'

'Well, you screeching isn't helping,' said Grace.

I kept imagining the blade piercing my skin and ripping through layers of muscle and fat. My stomach and legs felt icy cold. I couldn't forget Kyle's eyes.

'Thank goodness the hospital's so close,' said Grace. Her voice matched the rhythm of every gear change.

The world seemed to drift away from me. My eyes opened and closed without my control. My fingers, held tight at my stomach, felt as if they were in a hot, sticky porridge. The engine roared, and the wind moaned and whistled.

'Can't you go any faster?' said Sophie.

'Look,' said Grace. 'I'm driving, and it's all I can do to stay in a straight line.'

'I know, I know, I'm... sorry.'

I felt cold all over.

'He's shivering really badly,' said Sophie. 'Joel, say something.'

I seemed to emerge from a dark tunnel into the dazzle of the car with snow all around us. I tried to move, but an electric jolt kept me pinned to the seat.

'It hurts,' I said.

'It's alright,' said Grace. 'We're not far from the hospital.'

I felt her hand on my leg. She squeezed and some of her warmth flowed into me. I didn't dare look down again. The whole of my lower body prickled with pins and needles. I swallowed the sick feeling at the back of my throat.

'He's not going to, like, die, is he?' said Sophie.

'Look, blondie,' said Stark. 'Why don't you button it, it's not helping.'

'Well, it's your fault, anyway,' she said.

'You what?'

'You took us there.'

'There were no other fucking way.'

Silence.

'Who were those people?' said Grace. 'We were in trouble back there.'

'I told you,' said Stark. 'The residents. They're big, real big. Even cops keep away.' He tutted. 'That blow were worth a bloody fortune.'

'Stark,' said Grace. She hesitated. 'Mitchell... I just wanted to say thanks for, you know...'

I turned my head slightly and caught Grace's eyes searching for Stark in the mirror.

'Forget it,' he said.

'Yeah, I know, but you—'

'Look, I said forget it.'

Her face was full of questions. She shook her head.

'Just drive,' said Stark.

Concrete and discoloured snow conspired to turn the world grey. There were no birds, just an east wind gusting relentlessly. Huddled groups of people, hooded and bent, shuffled away from the city. My youthful disassociation from recent events was stripped away. I saw the whole of the country and all the people in it, trying to make lives for themselves, their children and those reliant upon them. Then there seemed to be the strata of people who had surmounted their physical needs and sought to control other people's lives and shape their aspirations and outcomes. I realised how hard it was to think for yourself, to stand back from culture and tradition and reach new, enlightened conclusions. I had no religion, although I knew Mum had a very personal faith, and I could see the benefit of a higher, objective moral force. It was a shame that superstition and prejudice were synonymous with the great religions of the world. If only we could distil the morals from each faith and create something new and free from ritual.

I was jolted against the door as the back end of the car spun in a slow-motion arc. Sophie screamed, and Stark swore.

'Shit,' said Grace.

A dog ran off the road with something in its mouth and disappeared into an alley.

'I thought you'd hit it,' said Sophie.

'Sorry, I just...'

The pain in my side came in red-hot pulses and spread around to my back.

'You okay?' said Grace.

I breathed in through my teeth and opened my eyes. 'Yeah, sort of.' I moved the hand covering the wound. A cold sweat burst on my forehead. I didn't know how much longer I could keep going.

10. Omens

I opened my eyes. Grace was talking, and the radio was on.

'Hospital, one mile,' she said. 'Nearly there.'

'Hang on in there, Joel,' said Sophie.

It felt as if there was a restless, fire-breathing dragon in my stomach. On the radio, a female continuity announcer spoke in a clear, relaxed voice.

'We can now bring you a special announcement from the Temporary Administration.'

Sophie pulled at the seat behind me, and I smelled the remnants of her perfume.

'Are these the people that have—?'

'Shh,' said Grace. 'We might miss—'

'Good morning. I am speaking to you from somewhere in the south of England.'

It was a man's voice—mature, educated. The acoustic sounded as if it was coming from someone's living room.

'Is this, like, going out now?' said Sophie.

'Can't you just listen?' said Grace, moving her hands rapidly up and down.

'I am part of a group of like-minded people who, despite having remained patient during these last, troubled years, have decided, reluctantly, to act. We call ourselves the Temporary Administration. We believe that our action is in the democratic and best interest of the peoples of this country. Let me be clear. By that, I mean everyone in this country. We have a figurehead, whose identity I cannot reveal at this stage, but is known to you all. At their instigation we have enlisted the help of significant sections of the armed forces, police and various media organisations. Throughout the country we have a network of trusted supporters who, like us, are not prepared to stand by and witness the ruination and debasement of this great nation and its libertarian values.

It was hard to take it in.

'It's just like that War of the Worlds radio broadcast all over again,' said Grace.

Sophie looked blank. Stark muttered something about *sorting them out.* Despite the pain, I bristled at the patronising tone of the man's voice.

'We have taken control of major sections of this country's infrastructure—notably power, water, telephony and the Internet. We have allowed gas to remain flowing so that the elderly and vulnerable can remain warm during this cold weather. It was necessary to interrupt power supplies to facilitate our plan, although we hope to restore electricity as soon as possible. We, The Temporary Administration, intend to oversee a transition period so that new elections can be held. As soon as these are in place we will disband. To ensure that order is maintained, we will enforce a curfew from six o'clock every evening until seven o'clock the following morning. The former government, its ministers and civil servants will face arrest when they return to this country.'

'I don't fucking think so,' said Stark.

'To those citizens who are directly opposed to our actions I say this: please understand that we wish to ensure that your voice is properly heard, that the democratic institutions of this country are respected and properly exercised. Fresh elections will ensure that we can forge a new relationship with our closest neighbour, The European Union.'

The man stopped talking, and there was a clicking sound.

'That was a broadcast by The Temporary Administration.'

Grace turned the volume control, but there was only hiss and the vibration of the engine. The man's words gathered around me and fell like poisonous rain in my mind, soaking me with their finality. I wanted it to be some kind of joke, a mistake, but I knew—really understood that we were in the middle of something momentous, something life changing. My knuckles bulged around my knees and I felt my young self slipping away from me like a shadow. If this was growing up you could keep it.

Sophie was crying. 'I just thought everything would go back to normal,' she said. 'You know, like, after a power cut. And now, well... oh, god. I just want to go home.'

'I don't believe a fucking word on it,' said Stark.

Grace's eyes were wide and focussed on the road. Her bottom lip trembled as she flicked the indicator. 'We're here,' she said. 'Let's just concentrate on getting help.'

Gritting my teeth, I pulled myself up in my seat. My breaths were short and rapid. We swung off the main road and onto the approach to the hospital. It was a whiteout. Every sign was encrusted with snow and ice. Power cables bulged and hung low with the weight of frost and every surface had a thick white hat. Huddled shapes moved along black meandering corridors of slush. Every road, every access point and parking area was filled with stationary cars.

'I think this is as far as we go,' said Grace. 'Joel, will you be okay walking from here to the E.D?'

I nodded. What choice did I have? We pulled up between two other vehicles, their doors open. Getting out of the car was a pain-drenched nightmare. I breathed in short, sharp bursts, but even with Grace and Sophie's help it was agony. Hot sweat bubbled on my forehead in defiance of the sub-zero temperatures outside. Sophie pulled my beanie low over her head so I could only see the lower part of her eyes. For a moment, all four of us stood by the car.

'I'm going,' said Stark.

The wind pushed tiny particles of ice into my face and eyes.

'What?' said Sophie.

'Yeah, you lot'll just slow me down.'

'Thanks a lot,' said Grace.

'I fucking don't owe you nothing.'

My fingers were brittle with cold as I held onto the car. Stark walked away from us with his back to the wind. He held up two fingers, turned and headed off into the sleet and mist. He never looked back.

11. The Walk

Sophie held out my beanie.

'Here—you could use this to...'

'Thanks,' I manoeuvred it over the wound. My hand was caked in blood but the bleeding had at least slowed. We walked. Almost bent double against the wind, we headed towards the whitened blocks of the hospital. There was no escaping the determined cold. Every breath forced frozen crystals to the back of my throat. I was a walking snowman with a burning fire in my side. There was no sign of Stark as we made our way along whitened pavements, past darkened bus shelters and bins. Snow and ice covered every sign, every gnarled tree and building. A few cars negotiated the slush-filled road and grey-white clouds seemed to hover just feet above us.

Sophie's purple boots weren't designed for snow. She took ballet steps and her arms waved around her. She took my arm. I wasn't sure who she was trying to stop from falling over. Grace walked a little way ahead, arms at her side.

'I'm glad Mitchell's gone,' said Sophie. 'He, like, creeped me out.'

The wind whistled around our legs. Grace turned her head.

'Why don't you call him Stark, like everyone else?' she said.

Sophie's grip on my arm tightened. 'No reason.'

Grace slowed. 'It's just that I heard—'

'Heard what?' said Sophie. She pulled at my sleeve.

'I seem to have touched a nerve,' said Grace.

'Stop it, both of you,' I said.

Sophie looked at me. 'Joel, I...' Her eyebrows flexed up and her eyes betrayed a complicated truth. I didn't want to hear answers to the questions that were forming in my head. Her fingers loosened their grip on my arm and then let go. A siren wail broke the glacial spell, the sound filling up the growing gulf between us. An ambulance appeared, its blue flashing light amplified by the all-pervading snow. As we came nearer to the wide, glass-fronted main entrance, ghostly, silhouetted figures watched from lighted windows in the upper floors. They had power. Concrete slabs, cleared of snow preceded automatic doors, which opened as we approached. On either side of the main doors people stood huddled, heads down with cigarettes hanging loosely in unsteady blue-white hands. Voluminous clouds of grey smoke billowed through flushed red nostrils.

Inside, the place was rammed. The main doors were like a giant mouth that had just feasted on hundreds of panicking women, men and children. Any second now they would be chewed, digested and conveyed to the innermost workings of the giant beast. At that moment, oblivion seemed an attractive proposition. A wave of sickening pain almost doubled me over.

'Let's stop,' said Grace.

'No,' I said, my breaths fast and shallow. 'Keep going. I'm okay.'

Sophie said nothing. Were those tears in her eyes? We joined the crush of bodies. Everyone was moving in different directions, not running exactly, but with impatient speed. Garish fluorescent lighting gave a nightmarish realism to the uniform white surfaces, and hidden loudspeakers pumped out echoed announcements competing with the assault of anxious voices. The strong smell of disinfectant failed to mask the thick, cloying odour of sickness and decay. Lights sparkled at the corners of my vision. Signs for Phlebotomy, Pain Clinic, and X-Ray South came and went. Where was everyone going? Two men were shouting at each other in the middle of the corridor. A boy of about nine, his face buried in his screen, stood unnoticed with his back to the wall. His thin face and twitching lips reflected colour after colour as he tapped the surface. He looked up and for a moment our eyes connected.

'I can't stand this...' said Sophie. Her words were lost in the barrage of sound.

We snaked, with Grace leading us, towards the lifts. A mass of people gathered around three sets of doors. We moved to the wall at the back, allowing people behind us to squeeze past. An elderly woman, smiling and leaning on a stroller, inched past us. Grace indicated with her head.

'Stairs,' she said.

I saw the relief on Sophie's face. With unspoken agreement we pushed our way through, wading through a sea of 'sorries'. Beyond heavy glass doors, it was another world.

'OMG,' said Grace, standing and breathing deeply one hand on her chest. 'That nearly brought on my asthma.'

Her words reverberated in the wide, open stairwell. With at least seven floors, it sounded more like a church, with a temperature to match. I shivered. The sound of unseen feet moving quickly on stone steps filled the air.

'It's never been this busy,' said Grace, her breath clouding before her. I caught a faraway look in her eyes, as if she were remembering something. I breathed through the pain in my side. Only when I moved suddenly did it give me an unexpected and unwelcome reminder.

'We need to go down one floor,' said Grace.

'You first,' I said.

I grabbed the generous wooden bannister and sucked in air with every step. Grace and Sophie matched every tentative movement. The, *I'm sorry,* message kept coming back to me, and a world of possibilities and explanations kept presenting themselves, over and over. The truth was, I didn't know where Mum and Dad were or what had happened to them. The logo—the burned message. The connection dropped into my mind. I tried to hold the thought, expand the context. A pin on a jacket, catching the light. Almost as quickly, the image and the certainty evaporated.

'Hey,' said Grace. 'Watch where you're putting your feet.'

At the next floor down, we pushed through double doors into a foaming river of tightly packed flesh. It was a living nightmare of bodies, noise and an unspeakable stench, like warm shit.

Sophie pinched her nose and Grace held the back of her hand up to her face.

We huddled together. The beanie pressed to my waist felt damp and sticky. White-coated wraiths with shadowed eyes wandered among the anxious throng. We were pushed from all sides. Someone hit against my arm and they turned to see who had made the noise. An older woman with skinny arms mouthed an apology before her heavily made-up face disappeared into the crowd. Grace's Afro, a little way in front, rose above the sea of heads.

I heard the gang at school, heard their words—taunting me. I remembered every word, every gesture. My head felt hot. I looked around—too many faces. Maybe all these people heard the radio broadcast? I felt conspicuous and vulnerable. There were other Black and minority ethnic people, but the vast majority were light-skinned. I was not a foreigner; this was my country too.

Up ahead, in what looked like a waiting area, a crowd of people, at least four deep, besieged a reception desk. Around it, and stretching to each distant wall, every chair, every surface was occupied. People stood in apathetic groups, jostled by an endless surge of bodies making their way further into the building. We moved to the edge of the crowd.

'This is impossible,' I said.

'Ridiculous,' said Sophie.

'Is there a queue?' said Grace, leaning in to a man immediately in front of her.

The man turned his head, looked Grace up and down, muttered something and looked away.

'Excuse me?' A middle-aged woman touched Grace's shoulder, her voice pitched above the background din. 'You need to get a ticket from over there. Yes, from that tall, white, box thing. They'll call you when they're ready.'

She raised her eyes to a ticker-tape style display above the main desk. The sign slowly spelled out that there was an *unavoidable delay due to unforeseen circumstances,* and that there was a waiting time of five to six hours. Pins and needles ran the length of my body. I put my hand on Grace's shoulder.

'Thank you,' said Grace, and smiled at the woman.

'Are you okay?' she said, pushing long, slightly greying brown hair away from her face. She wore bright red lipstick, which made her teeth look very white. She smiled easily.

'Yes... well... no. I'm fine, but my brother, he's been injured.'

The woman's eyes followed Grace's. Her mouth made an 'O' shape and her forehead creased.

'Oh, love,' she said. 'I see. I'm afraid you've a long wait ahead of you. It's beyond everything here today.'

'How long have you been here?' said Sophie.

'Oh, I've rather lost track of time,' said the woman, blinking and looking around, anxiously. 'At least three hours.'

'Oh, right,' said Grace.

'Well, I'd better get back. I was only stretching my legs,' said the woman. 'Good luck.'

Grace waved her hand—a little-girl wave that made me swallow. The woman turned and was quickly lost in the tide of people. Grace turned and breathed out through her nose. She made a fist and pressed it to her chest.

'Right,' she said. 'You both wait here and I'll get a ticket.'

'Alright,' I said, the throbbing in my side suddenly worse.

Grace nodded and tried to smile. She came over to me and gave me a careful hug.

'Ow, what was that for?' I said.

She shook her head. 'Nothing.'

She turned away and walked into the crowd. I could see the top of her hair as she made her way over to the far side of the substantial space. The thought of five hours in this place made my chest feel tight. I breathed deeply. Sophie stood with her arms folded. There was a tear near the collar of her shirt and her boots were stained and wrinkled. Her eyes wouldn't quite meet mine and her mouth opened and closed. I was about to turn away when she touched my arm.

'Joel?'

Her voice sounded like the Sophie I knew before. For a moment the surrounding chaos slowed and diminished.

'I couldn't really talk to you with, like, you know...'

With Grace around, I thought.

She extended her hand a short way towards me. My face must have said everything because she pulled it back towards her. She nodded.

'I came in the car because of you.' She put both hands over her face and let them fall slowly. She spoke through her fingers. 'I just can't seem to say the right thing.'

I felt something of how she used to make me feel. 'Look, Sophie,' I said. Maybe—'

'Don't say anything, Joel. Just don't say anything.'

She shook her head in the way that she did. It used to light me up, but right then I knew she was trying to hold it together. A man came and stood next to us.

'Actually, I think I might go to the loo,' said Sophie.

'Can't we just...' I sighed and watched her go. I leaned back against the wall, the pain once again uppermost in my mind. The man next to me bit his nails constantly, his eyes flicking nervously in all directions.

'The baby,' he said, without looking at me.

'I'm sorry?'

'It's come early.'

'Oh, I'm—'

'It were a bastard getting here.'

I looked at him and tried to find the right expression. A tinny announcement made him stop biting his nails. Where was Grace?

'Fucking hell, that's me,' he said, and shot off towards the main entrance, roughly displacing bodies in his wake.

I needed to think. I wanted perspective but instead was bombarded by a muddle of conflicting thoughts and ideas. I didn't dare imagine that Brexit would fail. It seemed impossible, and yet... something had happened today, something momentous, and I was part of it. I remembered the piece of paper from Mr Andreas' desk. Keeping one hand firmly over my stomach, I reached around to my back pocket and felt for the crisp square. It was still there. I took it out. It felt sharp and angular and pieces of ash fell away as I examined it. I was aware of a new feeling in my side, a kind of heat. Tiny prickles of light sparkled at the periphery of my vision. The noise and chaos receded a little as I unfolded the blackened sheet. In the full glare of the waiting area I could see more clearly the damage done by the flames. The logo was there at the top right-hand side, just as I remembered it—three letters within a black circle. In my mind's eye I could conjure the pin on a jacket, bearing the same logo, but every time I tried to see it more clearly, it seemed to move further from view. I looked again at the address. It must be right in the centre of the city, I thought. A secret library.

A sharp, jagged pain made me shout out and the feeling in my right leg seemed to melt away. My hand clamped shut, and the paper crackled and collapsed between my fingers. My other hand went to my side. It felt wet. I caught a flash of bright red blood. What an amazing substance, I thought, carrying oxygen to every distant part of the human body. The room tilted and buckled. I could feel the knife going in again, sharp and cruel. There were feet, lots of feet, shuffling in all directions. A man's face came very close to mine. His lips moved, but his voice came from some other distant place. I wanted to say something. I wanted very much to say something, but the effort... I couldn't quite manage it. I could see Mum and Dad on a blanket in the park and the wasp that refused to leave. They laughed so much—we all did.

12. Answers

Lights—bright lights—jarring metallic sounds and electronic punctuation. There were voices, many voices. Torn apart—danger—fear. Then darkness and a soft, thickened warmth. I was floating on a wave of cushioned air, removed from the world below. I knew where I'd seen the pin. My name. Someone was calling my name.

'Can you hear me?'

It was a voice I didn't recognise—a woman's voice. My eyes were shut and my lips felt dry and unconnected to my nervous system. I managed a low animal-like sound.

'He's awake.'

Sophie's voice.

'Joel?'

Grace.

I fought to open my eyes, but the light and colours overpowered me. I tried to prise my lids apart.

'He's moving,' said Sophie.

'Look, he's opening his eyes,' said Grace.

Then the older woman's voice again. 'Mr Durand. Can you hear me? You're in hospital, and you've had a small procedure. Do you understand?'

I commanded my neck muscles to obey me.

'He's nodding,' said Grace. I could hear the relief in her voice.

'It's the anaesthetic, it can affect some people like this,' said the older woman.

'Thanks doctor, Lavelle,' said Sophie.

'You're welcome,' said the woman. 'Just give him time, he'll be absolutely fine.'

'So the procedure went...?' said Grace.

'As well as could be expected. We don't have full resources at our disposal but we stopped the bleeding and as the knife missed any vital organs, we were able to stitch the wound. He will need further attention, but with proper rest he should make a full recovery.'

Someone was crying and there was a regular electronic beep from something close by. From further away came the rhythm of many feet and simultaneous conversations. The sounds grew suddenly louder, and I felt a new fluttering in my chest.

'There goes my pager. Don't tire him too much with conversation and see that he drinks plenty.'

I coughed and a torrent of words formed in my head as I pushed down hard on spongy material. I moved my eyelids and a dark, rounded shape silhouetted against bright lights filled my vision.

'Grace,' I said.

'Hey, Joel,' she said. 'Thank goodness...'

Somewhere, much lower down my body, a feeling began. It wasn't exactly pain, but it reminded me of something unpleasant.

'Don't try to... let me help you.'

I felt warm hands just under my arms. I opened my eyes, fully. It was so bright. I closed them again and squinted at the shapes in front of me. Sophie. Something about her and Stark. I knew it must be important, but I couldn't quite focus. Grace was standing next to me, and another woman wearing a white coat and glasses stood close by, her head down. She was writing on a clipboard. I blinked and saw other people walking close by in all directions.

'Where are we?' I said.

Grace was wiping her eyes.

'You're in hospital,' said the woman with the clipboard.

'Are we on a corridor?' I said.

They looked at each other.

'The wards are, like, full,' said Sophie.

'You were lucky to be treated at all,' said Grace. 'Apparently there's a code black here which means it's a proper emergency.'

Grace pushed another pillow behind my back, and I stopped straining to sit up. 'That's better,' she said. 'Just try to relax.'

I remembered the letter and then the pin. It was as if cold water had been poured over me. 'I had a letter.' I said.

'What?' said Sophie.

'In my hand, I had a letter. It's really important and—'

'Oh that,' said Grace. 'It was all burned and falling to bits, we thought you must have been trying to pick it up or something when you fell over.'

My eyes widened, and I felt a heaviness in my chest.

'You were in a right state,' said Sophie.

'Thank goodness that man was there,' said Grace, giving Sophie a withering look. 'He got the doctors there almost straight away.'

I wasn't interested in details. I reached for Grace's arm and put my weakling fingers around her wrist. 'But did you read it?'

Grace shrugged her shoulders.

'Look, this is important.'

'You're still, like, recovering from the anaesthetic,' said Sophie. 'You need to—'

'Really important,' I said, my voice loud enough to attract the curious looks of passers-by.

'Alright, I get it,' said Grace.

She leaned in a little. It was lovely to see her face. 'Yes, I read the letter, but I didn't—'

'The logo,' I said, squeezing her arm. 'Did you recognise the logo?'

'No, I—'

'Think, Grace.'

She shook her head. 'I don't know.'

'Dad's jacket.'

'What?'

'It was on a pin under the lapel, I only saw it because he pulled his jacket a bit tighter one morning on the way to work.'

'Yeah, so?'

'Don't you see? He's involved with this group in the letter. It's something to do with what's happened today, I know it is.'

The noises around me spun like a whirlpool with Grace and Sophie at the centre. I could only see their eyes.

'He looks a bit funny,' said Sophie. 'Do you think we should call the doctor back?'

'Look,' said Grace. 'Just let *me* deal with it.'

I instructed the world to stop spinning. I took deep breaths, closed my eyes and opened them again.

'I'm okay,' I said. 'And stop talking like I'm an invalid.'

'Well, you've been out of it for ages,' said Sophie.

Stark's grinning face appeared in my mind. I pushed it away.

'You never asked me where I got the letter,' I said.

I let go of Grace's hand and pushed myself up a little on the trolley. The pillows were soft and yielding and the dull ache in my side began to throb. The dragon was no longer sleeping.

'Aren't you going to ask me?'

Grace lifted both hands, and her eyes widened.

'Andreas's office?' she said.

'How did you know?'

'You were dreaming about it before you woke up. But so what?'

A prickle of irritation twisted my mouth. 'The logo, it was on the letter and on Dad's pin.'

'Sorry, I don't see—'

'There's this place in the city, right in the centre—a library. I think that's where they meet up.'

Grace shook her head. 'I think you've been through a lot and you've had too much time to think. It sounds like a conspiracy theory.'

'Oh, my dad's into all that,' said Sophie.

Grace rolled her eyes. 'Okay, so there's a library in town, it still doesn't mean Dad's involved in something.'

I propped myself up on one elbow. The dragon was definitely awake.

'So why did Mr Andreas just up and leave?' I said. 'The headteacher of a major school, with one-and-a-half thousand students. He walks out in the middle of a major emergency. The minute the power went out, or maybe even before, he tried to burn the paper I found, got up from his desk and left. Don't you remember Stark saying that he heard him on the phone, that Mr Andreas knew what was about to happen and to meet in the usual place? The usual place.'

Grace wrapped her arms around herself. 'I just can't believe that Dad would have any dealings with anything, you know—dodgy. He runs a restaurant for chrissake.' She pushed a hand through her hair, flattening it and letting it slowly spring back into shape. She had that distant look in her eyes.

'I think after today, I can believe anything,' said Sophie. 'You really think your dad could be, like, mixed up in all this?'

I nodded. The dragon breathed fire.

'You okay?' said Grace.

I ignored the burning flames.

'Think about all the things he's said recently,' I said. 'They were all about *not giving up*, and *its not over yet*. He always gave me the feeling that he knew something. It's weird, I never really noticed at the time. It was as if he knew Brexit wasn't the final word. It's hard to explain.'

We were in a hospital corridor, debating the future of our country, in our own bubble of discovery and realisation. I felt like I was growing up, fast.

'Actually,' said Grace. 'Now that I think about it, Dad was always telling me not to worry, that everything would work out. You know how he gives you those long looks, and it's hard to break away?'

I nodded, a slow empathetic nod.

'Maybe he knew, you know, that something would happen—at the last minute,' she said.

'There was that call he got on his office phone,' I said. 'You know, the one just after breakfast?'

'I missed that,' said Grace.

'You were upstairs. Yeah—he was definitely all weird after that,' I said.

'It's just like Mission Impossible,' said Sophie.

'Except, this is real,' said Grace, in her best *don't-be-so-ridiculous* voice.

'If the rally broke up,' I said. 'Maybe Mum and Dad have gone to this place?'

The sounds of the hospital filled the pause in our conversation. We looked at each other, each knowing what the other was thinking, each knowing what we would do next.

'*Dr Khan, Dr Khan to reception.*' The announcement reverberated loudly from overhead speakers. The owner of the voice sounded as if they were on the verge of panic. It was the trigger for action.

'I can walk,' I said.

'Really?' said Grace.

'But you've just had stitches,' said Sophie.

I could feel the strength returning to my body. I flexed my fingers, stretching them as far as they could go and then made fists.

'I just need some strong painkillers and I'll be fine.'

'Joel, you can't,' said Grace.

'Try me,' I said.

I pushed down and swung my feet off the trolley. The dragon was wide awake and moving around. The room wobbled a little and then slowed to a steady state.

'He's gone a funny colour,' said Sophie.

Someone cleared their throat close by. I lifted my head, my hands gripping the waffled blanket that covered the trolley. It was Dr Lavelle.

'Mr Durand—out of bed?'

She was not amused.

'We have to get to the city,' I said.

She jabbed the top of her pen against the hard back of her clipboard.

'I suppose telling you that you risk opening your wound, that you risk infection won't deter you in any way?'

I stared at her without moving a muscle. She pushed sleek, metal-rimmed glasses further up the bridge of her nose. Her eyes, framed by eyebrows as dark as her hair, were steady and serious. She gripped her bottom lip with her teeth and sighed heavily through her nose.

'And you can't persuade him, I suppose,' she said, looking first at Grace and then Sophie.

Sophie moved a little closer. 'I think the doctor's right,' she said. 'Why don't you stay here and—'

'Don't tell me what to do,' I said, my voice quick and low. 'You know why I have to get to the city.'

Sophie turned away, muttered, and folded her arms. Doctor Lavelle looked around and took a step towards us. I noticed the dark circles under her eyes.

'Between you and me,' she said. 'We've heard that the army might be about to arrive. They may limit who can come in or out. Also, you might want to leave by one of the side exits. We seem to have a group of, shall we say, more extreme members of the public gathering at the main entrance. They're after nitrous oxide ampules.'

Grace looked confused. 'What's—?'

'Laughing gas,' I said.

'I don't want to be trapped here,' said Grace.

'I really have to get back to work,' said the doctor, bending towards me. 'Mr Durand, if you take it easy, you will probably be okay, but don't do any lifting or anything strenuous. Here are some painkillers.' She shook a small box, covered with black and red typed letters, before handing it to me. 'Take two of these every four hours, okay?'

'Thanks,' I said. The dragon was sleeping again, but every now and again it changed position. 'One last thing, doctor. You can't prescribe Celexa, can you? You know, it's—'

'An SSRI used to treat depression. Yes, I know it well. I don't know who this is for, but I'm afraid we can't help you. I'm sure I don't have to remind you that with all this political uncertainty, supplies from the EU have suffered. It's all academic anyway as you need a prescription.'

Her eyes flicked between me and Grace. Grace lowered her head.

'I'm sorry I can't be more helpful.'

Grace nodded and glanced at me through lowered eyebrows. Dr Lavelle smiled, turned and was gone. Sounds and noise crashed into my brain. Grace was pacing in a small circle, the end of her thumb in her mouth. 'Where's this all going to end? It's one thing after another. That voice in my head—she's back. I want Mum.'

I pushed myself up, and off the trolley, standing with one hand on my temporary bed. The blurring in my head cleared and I noticed a strong smell of bleach.

'Grace, look at me,' I said. 'I've got this feeling, I can't explain it, but I think Mum and Dad are in the city, at this Library place.'

'But you don't know that,' said Grace.

I could hear the familiar catch in her throat. Sophie looked at me as if I was on something much stronger than painkillers. She put a hand on one side of her face and let her eyes fall. I took a few tentative steps towards Grace, relying on the stability of the trolley.

'Look, we can't stay here,' I said. 'Doctor Lavelle said—'

'Why can't we stay here?' said Sophie. 'It's warm, safe... at least for the moment.'

'Well, *you* stay here then,' I said. 'You've got your phone—you can sit around and wait for the 4G to come back on…'

Her bottom lip quivered.

'I'm sorry, I…'

'Just forget it,' she said.

Grace folded her arms.

'I want to find out what's going on,' I said. 'And I'm not waiting around for a group of right-wing thugs to rampage through here picking on people. And by people, Grace, I mean us. I'll walk all the way to the city if I have to.'

Grace breathed out through her nose and gave Sophie a scornful glance. Neither of them said anything. I hoped that something of my determination might flow into them. Either that or Grace might decide that she couldn't let me try such a foolhardy thing on my own.

'Grace?' I said. 'Are you okay?'

She nodded. A small, little-girl nod that made me swallow and I could feel a pricking sensation at the corner of my eyes. I extended an arm, and her head fell onto my shoulder. Her breath was warm on my neck, and her shoulders jerked in random spasms.

'It's alright,' I said. 'It's alright.'

'I was so frightened,' she said. 'I thought you were going to die.'

I put a hand on each of her shoulders and pushed her gently away from me. Her head was down and all I could see was a mass of hair.

'And what if we don't find Mum and Dad?' she said. 'Then what?'

Her breaths became faster.

'Grace, listen to me.'

She slowly lifted her head, and I saw tears, big and glistening on her cheeks.

'I think this Library is a safe place. I think that, somehow, Dad's part of whatever's going on. Maybe Mum is too.'

'Those drugs have messed you up.'

'I'm serious. Didn't you think they were acting kind of weird this morning? At least Dad was. Why was he so keen for us both to come to the rally?'

There was a loud crash from somewhere further along the corridor, and someone screamed. Every cell in my body froze. There was shouting—men's voices, and they didn't sound friendly. Someone yelled: *you can't go in there.*

Another crash was followed by what sounded like hundreds of metal objects spilling onto a hard surface. The commotion didn't stop and was getting nearer.

Fingers gripped my arm. I turned to see Sophie staring at the entrance on the far side of the vast space. Her eyes were wide and unblinking.

'There, by the door,' she said.

Stark stood framed in the doorway. His head moved in a slow semicircle as a shadowy scrum of youths in low-slung jeans, hoodies and caps swarmed past him.

'Actually, maybe it's not, like, such a great idea to stay here after all,' she said.

Grace stopped crying, and an unspoken momentum began. Other people were already beginning to move, their faces registering the beginnings of fear.

'There's a side exit down here,' said Grace. 'It'll bring us out into the car park.'

The pain came in pulsing waves. I shuffled as fast as I could, pivoting on my good side and breathing rapidly when the leg on my bad side touched the floor.

'You okay?' said Sophie.

I nodded, feeling cold sweat building all over me. I just wanted to lie back down on the trolley and stop the weird feeling that was gripping my stomach. People milled around, pushing in every direction. Something was bubbling up inside me, something that made my legs feel like jelly.

'Keep going, keep going,' said Grace. 'Do you think they saw us?

'I don't know,' I said. 'I don't think so.' Then I remembered Grace's hair.

All around us was the sound of laboured breathing and the dull clack of many feet on polished surfaces. We moved with common purpose.

'Come on,' said Grace, a wheeze in her voice. 'We're nearly there. Through this door.'

On the other side of an unmarked solid wood door, the noise level dropped, as did the temperature. No one followed us.

'How do you know about this?' said Sophie.

Grace didn't even acknowledge the question. She stood still, slightly bent forward, her hand on her chest. She fumbled in her pocket and pulled out her inhaler. She sucked and her eyes rolled back as she pulled it away from her mouth. I put two tablets on my tongue. They tasted dry and bitter.

'Who was Stark with?' said Grace.

Sophie shook her head.

I saw Kyle's eyes again—cold and empty.

'I'm not waiting around to find out,' I said.

Just ahead were glass doors and beyond them, the aching brilliance of the outside. I had visions of pitching over on the ice and opening my wound up. I had to remind myself that there was no choice but this course of action. Grace pushed at the doors and a sub-zero gale swept over us and into every gap in my clothing.

'Oh my god, we'll die,' said Sophie.

We huddled together. We were on a narrow, whitened path with a seven-storey wall behind us. The sky was a vivid blue and snow lay thick and unbroken over every visible surface. Beyond a line of tall, wiry trees came the distant roar of the dual carriageway. Flurries of crystals danced in the gusts that curled around our legs.

'If we go along here,' said Grace, 'and follow the edge of the building, we can get to near the main entrance and then take the road up back to the car.'

Sophie nodded. I kept my arms wrapped tight around my body, taking baby steps.

We slunk low and skirted the edge of the brick building, looking around the whole time. We took particular care near windows. There were no noticeable effects from the tablets, and a burning pain clawed down one side. Each step was a determined effort.

'You sure you could've walked into town?' said Sophie.

I was too busy being brave to form a reply and Sophie had to make do with a dismissive smile. Grace held up her hand as we neared the main entrance. We stopped.

'Where is everyone?' I whispered.

Grace shook her head. 'I'm not sure.'

There was a popping sound from inside the building. Even dulled and at low volume, it was unmistakable. We looked at each other.

'Let's get back to the car,' said Sophie.

We took the road that circled up and away from us before re-joining the main access road. As we neared the junction, there was a deep, sustained rumble. It came from towards the main road.

'Thunder?' said Grace, looking up.

The sound grew dramatically louder and was augmented by a repeated low squeaking sound. The ground trembled. Something big was coming our way.

'Stay close to these bushes,' I said.

From the imagined safety of a laurel hedge, a long cylindrical metal pipe slowly pierced our view. It appeared to float, and sunlight glinted on its grey, cold-looking exterior. Sophie gasped, and Grace's fingers curled around my arm. The full extent of the cylinder became apparent as the main body of a tank thundered into view. Its massive bulk was a jigsaw of metal plates and rivets, with a helmeted human head visible at the top, like a pink pimple on the hide of an angry beast. The tank rolled past us, continuing towards the main entrance, its relentless, stalked eye moving left and right. Behind it, following in tracks of crushed snow came a smaller armoured Land Rover. Low, and with tiny reinforced windows, it maintained a steady distance from its mightier brother.

'I've never, like, seen one this close before,' said Sophie. 'A tank, I mean.'

'So, the army *are* involved,' I said.

'Yep,' said Grace. 'This is where Brexit has led us. It's civil war.'

I straightened my back, and there was only a small amount of discomfort in my side. I felt colder than I'd ever been in my whole life, but adrenaline and pain were a potent distraction.

'But which side are they on?' I said.

Shouting began near the main entrance.

'Look, over there,' said Grace.

She pointed towards a group of people running across a snow-covered expanse. There was a sharp cracking sound, and one of them fell.

'Oh my god,' said Sophie. Her hand covered her mouth.

The others kept running. I could see a lone person pursuing them, but at this distance it was hard to see anything clearly. The single shape stopped, and another *crack* echoed between the buildings.

'This can't be happening,' I said. 'We've got to get out of here.'

My feet wouldn't move. Grace pulled my arm. We stumbled on, looking back the whole time. The tank moved close to the main entrance and stopped. The Land Rover moved closer still and dark figures spilled out of a rear door.

'There it is,' said Sophie.

Cocooned in snow, the car was exactly where we left it. I wondered for a moment if Miss Talland had noticed its absence from the staff car park.

'Thank goodness,' said Grace.

Distant shouts came from the direction of the hospital building. We were almost at the car when Grace stopped. I followed her eyes. On the far side of the car, in front of dense shrubbery, a shape was moving with a regular, rocking motion. Grace gestured with her hand for us to slow down. We edged around one side of the car and stopped. Before us, sat a teenage girl.

13. Sky

She was sitting on the back of her heels and her unusual shape comprised a giant rucksack and heavy-duty Parka its hood pulled over her head. I could just make out a mouth, its bottom lip prominent. She hadn't noticed us, or if she had, wasn't paying us any attention. She was rocking slowly backwards and forwards and was singing. No, it was a whimper. She was crying. Sophie approached and the girl fell backwards, her backpack supporting her. Her hood dropped back, revealing a fresh, youthful face framed by thick, long black hair. Her mouth opened as if to scream.

'It's all right,' said Sophie, showing both palms to the girl.

She stopped kicking her legs, and the rapid, panicky breaths subsided. Her eyebrows lowered a little.

'Are you okay?' I said.

The girl just looked at us and started crying again. She covered her face with her hand.

'She might be a student,' said Grace. 'From the university.'

'Or a tourist?' said Sophie.

The girl lowered her hand, revealing red-rimmed eyes.

'I'm not a tourist, I live here,' she said, before dropping her head again and her whole body convulsing with sobs.

Grace went over to her and put a hand on her shoulder. She recoiled and pushed ineffectively with her heels against the snow.

'Are you with them?' said the girl.

Grace shook her head. 'Who?'

The girl wiped her eyes with one swipe of her hand. Her face was red and blotchy.

'The people that forced me off the bus.'

Grace shook her head. 'I'm not sure why you'd—'

'When the news came through, they just threw me off.' Her mouth quivered. 'Like I was a piece of rubbish—something to get rid of. It was so humiliating.' Her head fell forward. 'I'm supposed to be at the airport, right now.' She looked up at Grace. Tears ran unchecked down her cheeks.

Grace crouched down. 'Look, we're nothing to do with those people.'

I managed a thin smile. 'It's complicated. We sort of borrowed a car from school.'

'*Stole* a car,' said Sophie, her arms folded. She stood a little further away.

'Don't you want to get up?' said Grace. 'You must be frozen.'

'Actually,' she said. 'I can't feel my feet.'

Grace stood up and extended her arm. The girl looked at her, removed her glove and took hold of her hand. She looked very unsteady at first.

'I've got pins and needles,' she said, brushing snow from the back of her coat.

'Where are your family?' said Grace.

'Oh, it's just me and my dad. My mum died two years' ago.'

Grace looked at a loss for words and glanced in my direction.

'That's... rough,' I said.

'Yeah,' said Sophie.

A massive bang from the direction of the hospital made us all jump.

'We need to get moving,' said Grace. 'Things are getting nasty over there.'

She looked over towards the cluster of hospital buildings. Above us, a lone seagull squawked, slicing through the air in a slow curve.

The girl moved forward. 'I'm Sky.'

'Hi,' I said.

'That's a lovely name,' said Grace.

'Thanks,' said Sky, for the first time the semblance of a smile flickering across her face.

'Weirdly enough,' said Grace. 'This is our car.'

She pointed at the roughly car-shaped blob of white in front of us.

'Really?' said Sky. 'If I believed in signs, I'd say it was meant to be.'

Grace started moving snow from the windscreen with big, sweeping gestures of her arm.

'Does your dad, like, know where you are?' said Sophie.

For a moment, Sky looked as if she might cry again, but she sniffed and raised her chin. 'He's at work so could be anywhere. I can't get him on my phone. I don't have a key for home on me and it's miles away anyway, on the other side of town. I mean, how would I get there?'

I stood up. Grace looked directly at me. She nodded her head, once, and her eyes flicked towards Sky. She raised her eyebrows.

'Er, you could always come with us?' I said, the words strung out and hesitant.

Sophie folded her arms and breathed out.

'Of course,' said Grace, wiping the side windows. 'You can't stay here. Maybe we could get you part of the way home?'

I couldn't read Sophie's expression. She walked to the other side of the bumper. 'You'd better, like, start the car,' she said, a chill in her voice.

'Right,' I said, trying to catch her eye but her expression had taken on a new and mysterious complexity.

'Where are you going?' said Sky.

I looked at Grace. 'Well, we're not sure, actually. We're trying to find a particular place, but we've only got part of the name. It's a library right in the centre of town. It's something like... LEY HOUSE LIBRARY.'

'Bramley House Library?' said Sky.

Blood thumped in my neck. 'You know it? Really?' I said.

'Yeah, my dad's a member,' she said, matter-of-factly.

I looked at her again, trying to gauge if she might be involved somehow. Sophie stood with her arms folded and avoided my eyes. Grace opened the boot, and Sky peeled off her backpack. It was agony getting back into the passenger seat. I felt hot and cold all over. I tried to distract myself with thoughts of food, but the pain was getting the better of me. I turned at the sound of raised voices coming from outside. Sophie had her back to Grace and did not look happy. She didn't seem anything like the girl I fell in love with.

It was late summer when I first saw her, properly. She was new to the school and we only had one class together. Every Friday afternoon, Mr Everitt in drama would get us to act out various scenes from well-known plays. I reluctantly stood opposite the new girl with the plummy voice and we both made the best we could of an excerpt from Romeo and Juliet. Mr Everitt insisted that when I said *Oh, that I were a glove upon that hand, that I might touch that cheek...* that I actually touch Sophie's cheek. She was supposed to say *Aye me!*, but when the moment came I sort of lost my place and kept my hand on her cheek. She raised her hand to remove mine, but the manoeuvre was never quite fulfilled. Her hand rested on mine and didn't budge. It took a few *Mr Durand—Miss Laing... please sit down*, requests to get us to disengage. Her eyes were extraordinary, and standing so close I examined the exquisite curve of her lips and trembled at their perfect symmetry.

I couldn't remember returning to my seat, but even though I was so moved by this encounter I didn't speak to her again for another two months. I didn't like her friends, much; they were always on their phones, whispering and giggling. But I could live with that. *She'll eat you up and spit you out, Durand,* my friends teased me. Then one morning she arrived at our bus stop—a blond superstar. Apparently, their house rental had ended, and they'd bought a place not too far away. Thus began a slow ballet of supposedly coincidental encounters. Her favourite was to arrive breathless, just as the bus was about to pull away. I would then almost single-handedly make the bus wait for her. She would smile and give me the look that sent my heart racing before getting on and always sitting a few seats away from me. The whole thing was ridiculous. Brexit changed everything.

14. City

The beast in my side seemed immune to the tablets. I shoved two more in my mouth. Without water, I tasted every bitter swallow. After a kangaroo start, Grace showed instinctive control over the car and resisted the temptation to show how quickly she could execute manoeuvres. Sky sat behind me with Sophie to her right.

'You never asked if Sky could drive,' said Sophie, a knowing edge to her voice.

Grace's eyes darted up to the rear-view mirror, and she shifted in her seat. I wanted to say something but couldn't quite find the right words.

Sky cleared her throat. 'It's okay. I can't drive.'

At the perimeter of the hospital grounds we came to a halt at the junction with the main road. Wide and still busy, we needed to take a right turn to the city centre. We stopped and waited, the indicator ticking. There were no gaps in the queue of slow-moving cars heading away from the city. On the other side of the road and beyond a high brick wall stood large houses sheltered by taller trees. To our left, drifting snow lay heaped against empty bus stops. Towards the city, traffic lights, standing like dead lollipops on a poorly iced Christmas cake, marked the curve of the road. The daylight had changed, and everything was tinged with blue.

The indicator blinked. Tick, tick.

'Hold on a minute,' said Grace. She looked distracted by something in her wing mirror. 'There's a group of people, right behind... oh god, they're running towards us.'

Tick, tick.

Still, no gaps. I tried to look all the way round, but it was too painful.

'Go on, Grace,' said Sophie, her voice rising.

'I can't. There are cars—'

Something hit the back of the car.

'They're throwing bottles,' said Sky. 'I think we need to get out of here.'

'Just push your way out, Grace,' I said.

'I can't, I can't.'

The back window shattered, and a rain of tiny fragments hit the back of my head. Sophie screamed. The car leaped forward, out towards the middle of the road.

'Keep the revs up,' I said.

'I know, I know,' said Grace.

A swarm of dark shapes moved across the snow behind us. Sky's quick, heavy breaths grew in intensity.

'They're catching us up,' said Sophie.

'Look out!' I said.

We just missed the front end of another car and a furious spinning sound came from the front and back wheels. It felt as if we were floating.

'Don't brake,' I said. 'Use the accelerator—power through it.'

Grace's eyes bulged, and her mouth opened. She leaned to the right and turned the steering wheel slowly and picked up speed.

'Oh god, oh god,' she said.

I looked around as best I could and saw dark shapes receding into the distance. Sweat turned to ice. Wind whistled through the car. Suddenly it was outside, inside. Grace's hair moved from side to side.

'Are you okay?' I said, turning my head towards the back of the car.

'There's glass everywhere,' said Sky. 'I'm fine, but... are you alright, Sophie?'

'No, I'm not.' She was crying. 'I can't take any more, I just want to go home. I wish I'd never got into this stupid car.'

'She's got a small cut on her head,' said Sky.

Sophie's sobs grew louder. I picked pieces of glass from my hair. My heart rate slowed a little. I turned the heating up full and made the vents blow the still-cool air into the back. Sky took her coat off and used it to fill most of the gap where the window should have been. The gale, ripping around the car shrank to a draught almost immediately.

'Hey, that worked,' said Grace.

'Nice one, Sky,' I said.

Sophie put both arms on the back of my seat and her head fell forward. She seemed inconsolable. We were heading towards the city. Deserted pubs, schools and mixed industrial units passed by in a frosty blur. The first and only petrol station that we saw looked more like a deserted car park. Empty vehicles, some with their doors open, were strewn everywhere. The entrance to the main shop was open, but inside was total darkness. Small packages and coloured items stained the blackened slush immediately outside. Like my fingers, my mind was numb. I wasn't sure what we were really doing. Chasing after an address on a scrap of burned paper? Some coincidence about a lapel badge? I swallowed. I tried not to think about what we'd do when it got dark. How were we going to get home?

'Joel, keep your leg still,' said Grace. 'It's getting on my nerves.'

I looked at my sister. She really was quite good looking, I suppose. Brown, unblemished skin, long eyelashes, and that pompom of hair. She looked more like a radical child of the sixties.

'Is anyone hungry?' said Sky, in a small, hesitant voice.

'Yeah, oh, my god,' said Grace. 'I am *so* hungry.'

'Maybe we could find somewhere on the way,' I said. 'You know, a shop or something?'

'But the power's out,' said Sophie, without lifting her head, her voice nasal and choked with sobs. 'Everything's out—the whole fucking world is falling apart.'

The steady hum of the engine and the rush of lukewarm air from the blowers filled up the empty silence.

'Actually,' said Sky. 'My dad packed me a lunch for the bus. We can share it if you like? He always makes loads.'

This was the first bit of welcome news in a long time. Grace positively bounced in her seat, and even Sophie looked up, red-eyed but expectant. I looked in the mirror.

'Sky, you're a wonder,' I said.

I caught a tentative smile.

'Thanks,' she said.

She rummaged in a small black package on her lap, and pulled out bottles, fruit and various chunky-looking items, some tightly wrapped in cling film.

'So, I've got water, an apple, a banana, cheese and pickle sandwiches on brown and a chicken leg. Oh, and some nuts.'

'And that was all just for you?' said Grace.

Sky smiled and her voice honeyed. 'Yeah, my dad's great.'

'How did your mum die?' said Sophie, wiping her eyes.

Grace turned her head towards me.

'Sophie,' I said. 'I don't think—'

'She had cancer.'

Sky spoke as if it was the most natural thing in the world.

'Oh, I'm sorry,' said Grace.

Sophie blew her nose. 'Yeah—that's like...'

Sky leaned forward with the water and touched my shoulder. 'You want a drink? Maybe your sister, too?'

'Thanks,' I said.

'Grace.'

'Hi Grace,' said Sky.

'Joel,' I said.

'Right.'

'So, where were you flying to?' said Sophie.

Sky swallowed and her eyes became distant. 'It was my big trip to visit my China mummy.' She let out a great sigh. 'My dad is travelling down tomorrow, or at least he was.'

'You might still make it,' I said.

Sophie thumped back in her seat. 'Joel, what is it with you?' she said. 'You need to get real, there's no point in pretending things'll be alright.'

My face flushed and my bottom lip hardened. 'Look Sophie, I don't know what *your* problem is, but I'm trying to stay positive. All you're doing is dragging the mood down. Lighten up, can't you?'

She leaned forward, her voice high and unrestrained. 'Lighten up? Really? With, like, all this shit going on?'

'Anyone like half a sandwich?' said Sky, her voice delicately pitched.

Sophie turned towards the window and folded her arms.

'Yeah,' I said.

'I'm pulling over,' said Grace. 'I can't drive this thing and eat at the same time.'

'Here you go, Sophie,' said Sky. She held out a sandwich.

Sophie turned and looked at her, hesitated for a moment and then nodded. 'That's great, yeah... thanks.'

'You're welcome,' said Sky. 'My mum always said that it was better to face whatever was bothering you, you know, to talk about it.'

Sophie bit into the sandwich and chewed her way through her response. 'I like the sound of your mum.'

Grace manoeuvred the car into a bus stop, its digital timetable, dark. There were hardly any cars on our side of the road, but a steady stream, their lights on, headed away from the city.

'Here you go, guys,' said Sky, handing us squares of thickly cut brown bread separated by layers of cheese and dark-looking pickle.

The flavour burst onto my tongue, and I joined the others in wordless expressions of pleasure. We chewed.

'Oh god, Sky, these are amazing,' said Grace.

'So good,' said Sophie.

'There's a chicken leg too, anyone want a bite?'

'Yeah,' I said, maybe a little too quickly. 'That is, if no one else...?'

Grace shrugged. Sophie said nothing. I bit into the white meat, my eyes closing in sheer pleasure.

'Now, that is just...'

'You can have my share,' said Grace. 'I'm vegetarian.'

A police siren sounded from somewhere behind us. Grace looked round.

'I count three cars,' she said. 'Coming our way.'

Blue light pulsed, reflected by every whitened surface.

'I don't think we should let them see us,' I said.

'What do you mean?' said Grace. 'It's the police, they'll help us.'

'I don't know, I just don't think anything's the same any more,' I said. 'Turn the engine off. I think we should duck down.'

'You're serious?' said Grace.

'Who, like, put you in charge?' said Sophie.

'Never mind that, now,' I said. 'Get down.'

Grace reached for the ignition, and a stunning silence filled up my brain. We all lowered our heads, Sophie last of all and with a petulant lack of urgency. Every scrape of fabric, every creak, dominated. Sky swallowed. Someone's stomach made a gurgling sound. The blue light grew in intensity and seemed to reach every corner of the interior. My side ached. I could feel the low hum of another car—several cars.

'This is ridiculous,' said Sophie.

'Shh,' said Grace.

I could hear a man's voice and then another but couldn't make out what they were saying. I felt the beginnings of fear—a cold sinking feeling in my stomach. Then a loud, distorted voice burst from one of the cars.

All units, all units, reports of a serious disturbance—Market Square, corner of Pelham.

The radio crackled and the voices began again, flowing over each other. Car doors slammed and engines revved. The blue lights slipped away. With the engine off, a numbing cold was already creeping up my legs. I rubbed my thighs and slowly raised my head.

'Well, they sounded like police to me,' said Grace, her breath already clouding in front of her.

'Can you turn the engine on, please?' said Sophie. 'It's getting super cold back here.'

'Sorry, I just thought...' I said. 'Oh, I don't know what I think anymore.'

'We're all feeling it,' said Grace. The engine came on and the blowers showered us with tepid air.

I realised that I was still holding the half-eaten chicken leg. I held it up. 'Anyone?'

'Yeah,' said Sky and relieved me of the greasy bone.

'Thanks again,' I said, licking my fingers.

I thought about school. The sudden darkness and the moment everything changed. It was more surprise than panic and the complete confidence that it would only be a temporary thing; that everything would just go back to the way it was. Who was really behind it all? I thought. I could see the pin, there under Dad's lapel. He covered it up the moment I saw it but he looked at me for just a little too long and I saw something in his eyes. Whatever it was, was pulling me towards the city.

Grace pulled back onto the main road. There were now only a few slow-moving cars travelling in the opposite direction.

'Look over there,' said Sophie. 'At that shop.'

On the ground floors of a row of dilapidated three and four-storey townhouses, were several shops. They were all boarded up except the one on the corner whose main door stood open at a weird angle. Boxes and their contents spewed out onto dirty snow, fanning out from the entrance. Two hunched shapes, hoods up over their heads, ran out and onto the street. Each cradled something bulky in their arms. Their pockets bulged. They paused, momentarily locked in the fascinated gaze of four teenagers. It was a millisecond out of time. Then, moving like ghosts, they ran up the street, slipping and sliding. They took a sharp right and were gone.

'So it's started,' said Sky.

'What?' I said.

'My dad got very negative about the world after Mum died. He said that society would collapse very quickly if there was any interruption of food or power.'

Grace and I did a *where the heck did that come from* double take.

'And you say I'm negative,' said Grace.

Sky sounded weirdly upbeat. 'Oh, it's not a downer, it's just practical. He said we should all be growing our own food, you know, not to be so reliant on others.'

'I guess so,' said Grace. 'But it does sound like doom and gloom, end of the world stuff.'

'Maybe,' said Sky.

'My dad says more or less the same thing,' said Sophie. 'Except he's on a paranoid trip. He drones on and on about how big business is, like, screwing us and that we're all like sheep. Only he knows *the truth*.'

I tried to imagine what would happen if the power never came back on. 'Well, it's just us now,' I said. 'We've got to stay positive and work together.'

Grace glanced in my direction and I realised that no pep talk would calm the deep worry I saw in her face. I touched my jacket pocket.

'My phone.'

They must have heard the near panic in my voice.

'Don't worry, I've got it,' said Sophie. 'Although there's still no network or 4G.'

She passed it over to me, taking care to avoid touching me. I let my fingers slide over its cool plastic surface. I pressed the home screen. It was just gone half-past two.

'We should be making a documentary or something,' I said.

'I'm out of power,' said Sophie.

'I've nearly got a full charge,' said Sky. 'Thanks to Dad.'

Her voice trailed off.

'What happened on the bus?' said Grace.

'I'm trying not to think about it,' said Sky. She had an unusual, clipped way of speaking. 'The people said a lot of bad words and made me get off. No one else on the bus said anything, I think they were afraid of them too.'

Grace nodded. I knew exactly what she was thinking.

'It must have been awful,' said Sophie.

'Can we talk about something else?' said Sky, turning to look out of the window.

'There's something up ahead,' said Grace. 'It's right across the road... cars, I think.'

'Slow down,' I said.

'They've, like, blocked the road,' said Sophie.

'This is how they stopped the bus,' said Sky.

Six or seven four-by-four vehicles were scattered right across the road, blocking the traffic in both directions. Dark-clothed figures moved about, some leaning into the windows of queuing vehicles. A group huddled around a glowing brazier, their hands outstretched. Bare pavement formed a rough circle around them. Sparks zigzagged up into the air, red against the deepening blue of the sky. From somewhere above us came the distinctive pulse of a helicopter.

'Okay,' I said. 'Something doesn't look right about this.'

Grace slowed to a crawl. 'Yeah—dodgy,' she said. 'They're definitely not the police, not dressed like that.'

'They look like a vigilante group,' said Sky.

'We should go back,' said Sophie.

'No,' I said. 'I think there's another way.'

I heard Sophie's weary exhale.

'Take a right here,' I said. 'If we go through the Park Estate, there are lots of ways in and out, they can't block them all.'

As we swung right, I saw one of the men take a keen interest in us. Just before he disappeared from view he placed a walkie-talkie against his ear.

The buildings changed from big detached mansions to subdivided terraces with lots of STUDENT ACCOMMODATION and TO LET signs. There were people walking about and everything looked almost normal. Dressed for the cold they had their hands in their pockets and heads down, following trails of blackened slush on the pavements. Even some shops looked as if they were open.

'It's almost as if nothing's happened here,' said Sky.

'Minus three, outside,' said Grace. 'Look, it says it, there.'

'Maybe the EU took all our weather, too?' said Sophie, with no trace of humour.

The estate was a warren of roundabouts linked by a baffling road network.

'I have no idea where we are,' said Grace.

'Don't worry,' I said. 'Just keep going.'

The roads and pavements emptied of cars and people, although there were plenty of car tracks and the snow on the pavements had a certain sharpness and rigidity, as if it were about to freeze.

'Hang a right here and we'll get to the middle of the estate,' I said. 'We can do a big loop around and then we should come out near the theatre, you know, the one with that round park next to it.'

'We saw some Shakespeare thing there with school,' said Sophie. 'It was mega boring.'

'My dad saw that too,' said Sky. 'He said it was inspiring.'

I could hear the longing in her voice—the worry and pain. I didn't need to see her face. I was trying not to think about Mum and Dad. I felt tingly and strange.

'Can anyone smell smoke?' said Sophie.

I sniffed the air. I could only smell damp clothes and hair, but there was a trace of something else. We were nearing the end of a gently curving canyon of old, imposing houses. We began to climb again, very slightly.

'I think I can, actually,' said Grace. 'Yeah.'

'Yuk,' said Sky.

It was a whiff of something, like a candle burning out and it was getting stronger.

'It's plastic,' said Sophie. 'Or rubber.'

We drove through a gateway with an old-fashioned five-bar gate.

'We did it,' I said. 'If you turn right here, the city centre is just down that way.'

The road we joined was on a gentle hill with generous pavements lined with mature trees. Tall, converted Victorian buildings stood resolute around us with gleaming gold and silver address plates on frost-covered pillars. Spaces, once occupied by cars, were snow-free and empty.

The moment when we would have to leave the car and decide what to do next was fast approaching.

15. No Way Back

The light was going. Snow and ice were turning a darker, more sinister blue. The edges of snowy peaks and waves of watery-looking crystals looked sharper, harder.

'I hope you know where this place is,' said Grace. 'This, library.'

Sky nodded. 'Yes. I know where it is.'

Sophie moved in her seat, like a princess on a pea. I turned my head. She was rubbing her hands together and sounded out of breath.

'Sophie,' I said. 'What's wrong?'

'I don't want to go to the city.'

Despite the pain, I turned around fully. 'But I thought you—'

'You can't make me.'

'Of course I can't, I wasn't even...'

Sophie wasn't Sophie any more. I felt prickles of irritation, an itch at the back of my neck.

'Oh, for goodness' sake,' said Grace. 'You've waited 'til now?'

'I should never have come. I want to go back.'

'Sophie,' I said. 'Calm down. We've come this far. If we can find this library, then it'll be a safe place. We're close, aren't we, Sky?'

Sky tilted her head. ' Yes.'

'Listen to you,' said Sophie. 'This is all, like, nonsense. You've dragged us here because of a stupid bit of paper. We're heading into trouble. I mean, can't you feel it? They were right, I should never have got mixed up with you lot.'

'You lot?' said Grace. Her whole body twisted in her seat, and her head looked ready to fly off. 'You're the same as Stark, aren't you? No, worse—you should know better.'

Sophie folded her arms. 'You're twisting my words, I didn't mean it like that.'

'Then what did you mean?' said Grace. 'Spit it out. I think racism is everyone's business, don't you?'

'Joel, don't let her talk to me like that. You know it's not true.'

I moved my hand towards Grace. 'Actually…'

The temperature in the car dropped to zero and continued to fall. No amount of heat from the blowers could displace the increasingly bitter atmosphere.

Grace's eyes were fixed and staring. 'It's just like all those politicians said nothing racist during the Leave campaign. They just nudged everyone in that direction, stirred them up. Believe me, I should know.'

There was a catch in her voice. I touched her arm, but she pulled away and stared ahead, glancing repeatedly in the mirror.

'Honestly, I—' began Sophie.

'Grace,' I said. 'I don't think Sophie would say anything—'

'You're sticking up for her?' Grace hit the steering wheel hard with both hands and let out a cry.

'Maybe it was just a bad choice of words?' said Sky. 'Maybe take a—'

The car jolted.

'What was that?' I said.

'How should I know?' said Grace, close to tears.

I scanned the dash. The car jerked forward and then slowed down.

'Give it more revs,' I said.

'I… I can't…' said Grace. 'Stupid car.'

The car shuddered and slowed dramatically. Grace steered towards the kerb but the engine had already cut out. We stopped. Dead. The blowers and lights went off and on again as Grace turned the key in the ignition. Nothing. Graces knuckles whitened on the steering wheel and her chest heaved as if she'd run a hundred metres.

'What's wrong?' said Sky. 'Why have we stopped?'

'I think we're out of petrol,' I said. 'This is as far as we go.'

'This is all my fault, all my fault,' said Grace. Her cheeks glistened, and her bottom lip trembled. 'Shut up, won't you?'

'Grace, who are you talking to?' I said.

'Don't touch me.' She pinched the flesh on her arm and raked it with her nails. Her head fell forward and hit the steering wheel. She started to cry. 'Just leave me alone.'

There was someone else in the car, some unseen malicious entity. We had to get those meds, and fast.

16. Schism

Leaving the car was like walking into a freezer. Even with all my layers, the fingers of cold seemed to find their way to skin. It was a welcome distraction from the pain in my side. It was dusk, and without street lights the concrete world was a grim, unrelenting grey. Sophie got out last but only took a couple of steps away from the car before stopping. She looked back the way we'd just come and then towards us. The wind howled, throwing spirals of off-white crystals up to the unseen tops of oppressive buildings.

'Are you coming?' I said, my words jumbled by an uncontrollable shiver.

Sophie pulled the lapels of her coat tight against her neck. She shook her head but then took a step towards us, and then another. A complex mix of emotions rushed over me: relief, regret, anger. How easy everything was only twenty-four hours' ago.

'You okay, Grace?' I said.

She'd stopped crying. Her eyes met mine. I felt as if I'd distracted her from something that demanded her full attention. Immune to the cold, she tilted her head and her forehead creased.

'Sorry... yes. I think so. Is Sophie coming with us?'

I nodded. Grace sighed.

'I think I lost it back there.'

'Yeah.'

'I should say something to her.'

I shook my head. 'I don't think she's in a good place at the moment.'

Sky pulled her rucksack from the boot as Sophie approached. Sophie's bottom lip trembled.

'Just don't say anything,' she said. 'I'm only coming because I haven't really got much choice. Have I?'

Grace registered no sign of emotion. I couldn't think of a good answer. The wind seemed to pull my thoughts away as fast as I could think them.

'How far to the library?' I said. I struggled to ignore the now constant throb in my side. I willed the stitches to hold.

'About ten minutes,' said Sky. 'You will slow us down a little.'

'Okay, thanks for that,' I said.

With Sophie trailing behind, Sky led us through the whiteout, past tall office blocks and abandoned cars reduced to mounds of snow. Darkened shop frontages heightened the surreal atmosphere and it felt as if we were the only living people in the whole city.

'I can smell it now,' said Sky. 'Someone's burning tyres or plastic.'

The road widened and multi-storey buildings glowered at us with cold, empty looks.

'I think it's trying to snow again,' I said.

A few stray flakes heralded a wave of thicker, more substantial snowflakes.

'What are we doing?' said Grace.

'We're trying to help you get well,' I said. I put an arm around her, but she seemed almost not to notice.

It was getting late. We had to find this place before we lost the light. I didn't want to think about the word, *dark*. Just the thought of it made my chest feel tight. Each step felt as if the wound in my side was being prised open. The pain made me catch my breath and sweat filmed on my neck and back. I let my fingers find the area of the wound and held my breath as I raised my hand. There was no blood. I breathed out.

Sky walked with Grace so I slowed down and let Sophie catch me up. She glanced at me, her downturned mouth unmoving. Not a flicker of warmth or interest. She may as well have looked through me.

I rubbed my hands together. 'Hey.'

'Hey,' she said. Her eyes looked everywhere except at me.

'In the car, that was... unfortunate,' I said.

She stopped and turned to look at me properly, her blue eyes as cold as the snow. She looked away and made a circle in the snow with the toe of her shoe.

'I'm just sick of it all,' she said. 'You, your sister... Brexit. But I'm like, stuck with you, and there's nothing I can do about it.'

I felt the chasm between us and I wasn't sure that I wanted to bridge it. I knew then that we really were finished.

'I'm sorry, Sophie.' I said. 'Really, I am.'

She looked at me and for a moment her face softened. 'I liked you, Joel. I really did. You were different to the others.'

She shrugged her shoulders, dipped her chin and tilted her head away from me. I put my hand on my side and tried to walk away without limping. I didn't want to feel. Maybe I did love her? Why else would I be shaking and my eyes leaking salty tears? Grace blinked when she saw me and shook her head.

'You look like shit,' she said.

I was too tired to pretend.

'I think that's it with me and Sophie.'

'Oh.'

I nodded. I wanted to cry, to really cry. I took a deep breath.

'Is it because of me?' said Grace. 'You know, what I said?'

I shook my head. 'No. I don't think we're right for each other. It's just taken me a long time to figure it out.'

'I'm sorry,' said Grace. 'I didn't exactly help, but she wouldn't leave me alone.'

'You mean the voice, don't you?'

She nodded. 'It makes me see things that aren't there.'

'Sophie's not that bad,' I said.

Grace looked at me with mild, *oh-come-on*, disapproval. 'I'm sorry, Joel,' she said. 'But I never trusted her. There was always something a bit...'

'What?' I said.

'Well, you know. Uber-rich white girl flirts with working-class Black boy.'

'You know how to make me feel special,' I said.

'I shouldn't say anything. I mean, hey, you might get back together?'

I pulled my, *if hell freezes over,* face.

A smoky haze swirled around the buildings. The burning smell was stronger.

'We're close,' said Sky.

She pulled at the straps underneath her arms, her backpack stuck to her like a needy parasite. Sophie followed at a distance as we headed down a short lane. She was with us, but not with us. A sudden wind forced powdery snow between our legs. Embedded within the moaning whip of the gust was another sound, just audible. It seemed to come from beyond the high wall of buildings opposite.

'It sounds like a football match, or something,' said Grace.

There it was again, an anguished cry, the sum of many voices. Sophie stopped and put a hand to her mouth.

'I can see people,' said Sky.

A blur of huddled shapes in the far distance were running towards us. From around the corner behind them came another, larger group. They were running too.

'It looks as if they're...' said Grace.

'Chasing them,' said Sky.

An animal cry burst across the road.

'In here,' said Grace.

We followed her under the substantial awning of a tall building, ducking down behind a low boundary wall. Sophie hesitated.

'Get down,' said Grace, pulling at her sleeve. I had to kneel, as I couldn't bend my waist. In the dull, near-darkness I could see the outline of Grace's head, the muted colours of Sky's hat and a few feet beyond, Sophie's eyes burning in the gloom—two pale circles of light holding me in an unrelenting gaze. I looked away and listened, the smell of burning, stronger still. A scream began and continued. It grew in intensity and seemed to come from all around us. There was a thump, and it stopped.

'Oh, god,' whispered Grace.

Shouting began all around us, the words indistinguishable. The violent sounds bounced between the buildings, rising in intensity. Rage. Frenzy. There was murder in the air. I could feel it, bitter in my mouth, carried on every new breath. Fingers tightened around my arm. I couldn't feel my knees, but I didn't dare move. The hungry wind, reached inside my jacket, finding my back and neck.

'Come here, you fucking—'

The voice was so close—a woman's. Then another voice—higher.

'No!'

The fear was like a virus, running rampant through my body. I could feel it working through my legs, stripping them of bone. Blood thumped in my ears, and my breaths were short and fast. There was the sound of someone straining, as if they were lifting a heavy weight.

'Traitor.'

The first woman's voice again. I could feel the clenched teeth—hear the spittle. A low sustained gargle, then a dull slapping sound, as if something were hitting the snow. I was stone. Someone, I think it was Sky, was crying.

The voices became jeers. Someone laughed. They diminished in volume until all I could hear was the wheeze and crackle of Grace's breathing.

'Have they gone?' said Sophie, her voice a tremulous whisper.

'I'm not sure,' I said. 'I think so.'

'I knew I shouldn't have come,' said Sophie. 'Oh god, that was horrible.'

'What just happened?' said Grace. 'Where are the police?'

Sky spoke, her voice punctuated by sobs. 'I thought they were going to find us. I thought...'

Her head fell forward into her hands. I put my arm around her. Sophie was off my radar.

'Hold on,' I said.

Still on my knees, I moved towards the edge of the wall and looked around. I couldn't see anyone. Distant echoes and sounds reverberated around the brooding canyons.

'It's clear,' I said. 'Come on.'

Sky's phone blazed a pool of light in front of her. 'What's that?'

About six feet away, an angled shape lay in the snow. It didn't move. As Sky moved her torch, I could see a bright red halo around one end.

'Oh, my god,' said Grace. 'Is that...?'

Sophie's hand flew to her mouth. I could see her lips move behind trembling fingers.

'Turn it off,' I hissed. 'Sky. Turn it off.'

It was a nightmare world of cold and shadows. The image burned in my retina. I stood up, ignoring a stab of pain, and limped over to the figure on the ground, looking around the whole time. I knew what I'd find. I pressed my home screen, and the faint glow illuminated the side of a woman's face. Her hair had fallen in irregular shapes over her still, pale cheek, but it was the eyes that held me in their sightless gaze. I reached out to touch her skin but stopped. I knew she was dead. The circle of blood beneath her head and chest looked thick, like red custard. I felt hot all over and tried to swallow. The contents of my stomach were suddenly in my throat and formed their own steaming pile in the darkening snow. I coughed and spat out the remains of the vomit. My stomach tried to push up more, but there was nothing left. I felt a hand on my shoulder. I turned. It was Sky. I pulled away.

'I'm alright,' I said. 'It was a shock.'

My hands wouldn't stop shaking. I took one step and then another, finding my strength again. Sky stayed at my side.

'You've never seen a dead person?' she said.

I shook my head.

'They can't touch her now,' she said.

Grace and Sophie were looking the other way when we approached them, their body language uncompromising.

'What are we going to do?' said Grace, her face hidden in shadow.

Sophie's eyes blazed red. 'Are you serious?' she said. 'We should turn around and get the hell out of here.'

'Get out to where?' I said. 'Back to no food and no power?'

'Well, it's not much better here, is it?' she said, her voice rising. 'There's, like, a dead body right there and we could be next.'

'All the more reason to get to the library,' I said. 'We'll be safe there.'

Sophie took a step towards me. 'Listen to yourself. All this library crap and based on what—a stupid scrap of paper?'

I could feel Grace's eyes on me.

'Admit it' said Sophie.

'I... I've just got this feeling,' I said.

Sophie turned in a full circle, her hands waving theatrically through the frigid air. 'A feeling? Oh, now we're here on, like, just a feeling?'

'No, it's more than that...'

'Stop shouting,' said Grace. She covered her face with her hands.

'Look,' said Sky. The tone in her voice made us stop and take notice. 'The library is on the other side of this road down that alley. We could be there in two minutes. Why not go there, as you've come this far?'

She pulled at the straps on her backpack, raising it higher.

'Who asked *you*?' said Sophie.

'Leave her alone,' said Grace. 'You'd be starving if it wasn't for her.'

A hot anger cleared my head—crushed the pain.

'Sky's right,' I said. 'We've just witnessed a murder and yet here we are standing around arguing. We're not kids any more. It's getting dark and we're going to the library.'

I didn't wait to see their reaction.

'Sky,' I said. 'Lead the way.'

17. Rally

A huge cheer rang out. A dull glow coming from the city centre turned the edges and fronts of buildings blood red. Smoke flecked with fiery embers rose in wide columns into the blue-black of the cloudless sky. I could see a star, and another. It was going to be a cold night.

'That sounds like many thousands of people,' said Sky.

I held my side and drew a sharp breath. 'We should maybe cross this road a little further down?'

'Yes,' said Sky. 'We'll be less exposed.'

We didn't need our phones to see where we were going. A ghostly light from the newly risen moon bathed the sea of snow at our feet, turning it into a luminous carpet. We kept our heads down as a few cars went by, heading north. They didn't slow down. We reached the other side. The acrid smell was getting stronger and the chorus of voices, louder. We walked under the portico of a darkened restaurant, its plate-glass windows smashed and glass scattered across the wooden floor inside. A curtain rail hung at a crazy angle, supporting ripped fabric. The wind casually lifted a shredded piece of material and snow crystals blew into the murky interior.

We kept going, staying close to the buildings, shuffling from shadow to moon shadow. Fear was our silent companion. I saw danger in every dark corner, every gust of wind. The pain in my side was constant, but I breathed through it. The air was super cold at the back of my throat. Sophie followed at a distance, every laboured step a reluctant contribution to the journey. My mind was elsewhere. I could sense that we were nearing something, something important.

'It's just down here,' said Sky, her backpack bobbing up and down in front of us.

'It looks very dark,' said Grace.

'At least we won't be seen.' I said.

It was as if we stepped out of our world into another. Buildings rose up on either side of us like sheer brick cliffs. High, frosted windows tinged with reddened frost interrupted the bleak façades. The sky was a thin sliver of blue, high above us. I pressed the side of my phone and the home screen came on, its pale light giving some indication of the ground beneath us.

'I never knew this was here,' said Grace.

'Me neither,' I said.

'There are lots of off-the-beaten-track places in the city,' said Sky. 'You just have to know where to look.'

Odd shapes and deformations softened by the snow slipped into shadow behind us. Every footstep crunch, every small, hollow sound was stretched and thinned. At the far end, the walls came together like a pincer with a slash of ruddy orange beginning at the bottom and gradually fading to brown then grey and finally black.

'I don't like it,' whispered Sophie, her words spilling out on tiny ice crystals.

'We're nearly there,' said Sky.

'Shh,' I said.

The smell of burning was stronger and the swell of voices rolled above and over us. Shadows within shadows shifted and twisted. My heart beat faster. Then another sound, one I didn't realise was there, stopped. I flashed my torch, and at ground level, dozens of pairs of red eyes shone back at me. From in front of me I heard a gasp and the beginnings of a scream. An enormous bang came from beyond the end of the alley and the ground in front of us came alive. A wave of black, undulating shapes moved over the snow towards us. There was nowhere to hide. The light from my torch caught the shiny brown of their backs as they moved almost noiselessly between our legs—a filthy sea of warm flesh. Grace stood, eyes closed and mouth open, her face tilted upwards. Her hands were tight fists, moving quickly back and forth. The ordeal lasted only a matter of seconds.

Sophie jumped around on the spot, brushing her legs and feet with her hands. 'Oh god, that's just the most disgusting thing I've ever...' She shook every part of her body.

'That was gross,' said Sky.

The shouting from beyond the end of the alley intensified.

'Let's get out of here,' said Grace.

'Come on,' I said. 'I don't want to be here for a second longer than I—'

We walked past what had held the interest of the swarm of rats. Lying between red snow and scraped earth, I could make out a leg and then a snout. The rest looked like something from a horror movie.

'I can't look,' said Grace.

'I think it was a dog,' said Sky.

'How can you be so matter-of-fact?' said Sophie, a cry in her voice. 'Don't you feel anything?'

Sky's head turned almost in slow motion, and her eyes rose to meet Sophie's. Sophie looked away. Sky pulled at the straps on her backpack, forcing it higher still. She walked ahead. The image of the mangled, half-eaten corpse burned in my mind. I wanted to cry.

We neared the end of the alley. Sky was leading, followed by Grace and then me. Sophie was last. Head down and arms folded, she muttered to herself. The wind blew cold and hard in our faces. Sky held up her hand, and we came to a ragged stop.

'Okay,' she said. 'The library is down there on the right, with the square further on, round the corner.'

From the darkness of the alley I could see that every shop within view was smashed to pieces, with glass and contents spread over the grey slush of the street. Overhead, above the dark tops of the many-storeyed, mediaeval buildings, burning embers jumped around the night sky. The dull roar of voices was even closer, just beyond the end of the street.

'Get back,' hissed Sky. 'There are people coming.'

I heard the stamp of many feet and raised voices. They were approaching, fast.

'They mustn't see us,' said Grace.

We slunk back into the shadows. I swiped my torch off. Shapes flashed by, just feet away from us, their rasping breaths fast and urgent. We were invisible. I was ready to move when another group of men and women ran past, each carrying sticks, held high above their heads. They made a collective sound that was animal—primeval. A flash of yellow. I gasped. The woman at the back was slower than the others. I knew the shape of those shoulders, the sound of that voice. With my hand pressed to my side, I stepped out of the shadows into the street. I shouted her name.

I could scarcely believe that the word had left my mouth. It reverberated to the very end of the street and up to the highest rooftop. Like some magic spell, it brought the woman to an abrupt halt; the stick held high in her right hand, challenging the sliver of moonlight that illuminated the centre of the road. She turned around, the stick beginning a slow descent towards the ground.

'Mum?' I couldn't disguise the yearning in my voice and took a step towards the woman standing transfixed in front of me.

Other people ran past, oblivious to us. The stick fell from Mum's hand. I wanted to laugh, cry and scream, all at the same time. She was still wearing her grey trousers but there was no sign of her jacket and her thin yellow top was ripped and stained. Her hair was all over the place and her face was sweaty and covered in dirt. There was a cut above her eye with dried blood around it. But it was the expression in her eyes that made me catch my breath. They were wide, and it was almost as if she wasn't really seeing me, but just hearing my voice. I walked up to her and touched her arm. It was freezing cold.

'Mum.'

Her eyes flickered, and her mouth opened and closed. She breathed out a massive sigh, and her hand went to her mouth.

'Joel? Joel.' She said my name over and over again almost as if she was waking from some deadly enchantment. Saliva bubbled in the corner of her mouth. She raised her arms. Grace ran past me and threw her arms around her, burying her head in her shoulder. Mum's eyes closed, and a hand came up to the back of Grace's head. Tears ran down her face. 'Mum! Oh, Mum.'

18. A Reckoning

Mum wiped away tears and snot with the back of her hand. Mascara ran from her eyes.

'You've got to go back—get out of here,' she cried.

I tried to speak but Mum shook her head. Her eyes bulged.

'Listen to me. You don't know what's going on. You're not safe.'

She pulled us away from the flow of people, back towards the wall. Her hands shook and she kept looking over her shoulder. 'Why won't you listen?' she said. 'You've got to go, now.'

People were running past us. I wanted to ask so many questions. My heart felt as if it was about to explode. Mum cried again and hugged us.

'Oh, my darlings. Just to know you're safe.'

There were shouts from further along the street. Mum seemed immune both to the noise and the cold.

'Mum, what's wrong?' I said.

She shook her head and turned, her eyes following the lines of raised hands. They were chanting: *enemies of the people.*

'Mum, you're scaring me,' said Grace.

'You're coming with us,' I said.

I indicated to Grace. I took hold of one arm, and Grace held the other.

Mum's face twisted in a look of horror, and she stiffened. 'No.' She dug her heels into the snow and struggled. 'Let me go. Let me go.'

'Mum, Mum,' I said. 'Where's Dad?'

'Yes,' said Grace. 'Where is he?'

Mum stopped moving. Her features rippled, as if consumed by a molten, violent force. She breathed through gritted teeth, curled back her lips and spat out her answer. 'That man... liar... liar.' She tried to break free. She was strong.

'Mum, what are you—?'

'I need to follow the others...'

Another boom came from somewhere towards the square and a massive cheer followed. She stopped fighting us.

'What happened this morning?' I said.

'Did you get the medication?'

'Where's Dad?'

'Aren't you cold?

Mum took rapid breaths through her nose and her eyes rolled in her head.

'Hold her up,' said Grace, 'I think she might faint.'

People ran by us. They were shouting, everyone was shouting. The feeling was like electricity. Something burst in the sky above our heads, and for a moment, everything turned blue. I could see them, like lemmings. The darkness that followed seemed deeper, more absolute. We were all moving towards a vast cauldron, brim-full of fire and malice.

'That's it, Mum, come on,' I said.

'Joel, what the hell is wrong with her? What's happened?' said Grace.

'I don't know.'

I could hear the chant, louder now: *enemies of the people.*

Mum's legs gave way beneath her.

'Stop. It's here,' said Sky.

We veered into an old recessed doorway, just removed from the incessant jostling and noise. At the end of a short hallway was another door. The moment the outer door closed, the noise stopped. It was as if someone flicked a switch in Mum's head.

'Mum, are you okay?' I said, and took hold of her hand.

She opened her eyes, wide. I saw fear and confusion.

'Joel... Grace, it's been terrible. I thought I was losing my mind. I can't tell you how good it is to see you.'

'Mum, tell us what happened,' said Grace.

She raised her head, and the tears stopped. 'Never mind about me. Why aren't you at school? How did you get into town?'

'It's a long story,' said Grace. 'When the power went out, Joel borrowed a car and we made it here.'

'I've got your tablets,' said Mum. 'They're in my jacket pocket.'

'Mum, you're not wearing a jacket,' said Grace.

Mum's hand went to her mouth. She looked around and then back to us. She shook her head.

'It's alright, Mum,' said Grace. 'Honestly, I'll be fine.'

'But you need them. How could I have been so stupid? Where is it? Where's my jacket? I was wearing it when...' Her face dropped. 'I've seen things that I can't unsee.'

'Just tell us,' I said.

Mum's fingers trembled as she touched her bottom lip.

'We'd just left the Pharmacy and your father; he said he had something to tell me. Well, you know how he's been lately—I didn't know what to think. There've been these text messages and...' Her breaths became faster and her mouth wobbled. The tears came again, and her hands balled into fists. 'He told me about this thing they planned, him and the others, against Brexit. I was so upset and angry. I told him, straight. *You can't be serious*, I said. But I could see it in his eyes. I knew it was the end of everything. He killed our marriage there and then. I just don't know who he is any more.'

'So it's true, then?' said Grace. She looked as if she was on the edge of a cliff, staring into the abyss.

'Yes.'

My hand jumped to my side, and I couldn't control my face.

'Darling, what's the matter?' said Mum.

'Oh, it's nothing.'

'Grace, tell me the truth.'

Grace opened her mouth. Her eyes met mine.

'I got in a fight, that's all,' I said.

Mum raised an eyebrow. 'Is it bad?'

'I'll survive. Look Mum, we just want to know why you're... why you're like this.'

She looked around. 'Where are we?'

I looked at Grace and then back to Mum. 'Did Dad say anything about a meeting place?'

Mum closed her eyes and pressed her lips together. 'Yes. He wanted to take me there, but I wouldn't go.'

'Well, this is it,' I said. 'At least we think it is.'

Mum opened her eyes and put her hand to her mouth. 'This is the Library?

'Yes,' said Sky.

Mum put her hands out, palms first, as if warding off an unseen enemy. 'I'm not going in there. I don't want to see him. In fact, I want nothing to do with him ever again. I know he's your father, but he's a liar. Everything we stood for, everything we built—gone.' Her voice broke.

'Mum, we're not even sure if he's in there,' I said.

Grace put her hands over Mum's outstretched arms and gently pushed them down, nodding and maintaining eye contact the whole time. Mum's eyes narrowed and the corners of her mouth turned down. When she spoke, her voice was low and calm but with an edge of steel.

'You're all going to have to choose a side.'

19. Portal

'How do we get in?' said Grace.

Sky pulled off her backpack and stood on tiptoe, pointing her phone torch up at the ceiling. 'There's something here, but I can't reach it.' She looked at me.

I pressed down on my stitches. 'I can't stretch that far.'

'I can,' said Grace, moving forward and reaching up to a featureless silver rectangle. Her fingers found an edge that yielded a little.

'Flick it open,' said Sky, still holding her phone up. 'Try one of those buttons.'

'Here goes,' said Grace. She reached up and pressed. 'Hello?'

Nothing. She let go, but kept her arm in place. She looked back at us.

'Press it again,' I said.

Cold sweat pooled on my forehead, and a trickle meandered down the side of my face. I clenched my teeth, and my breaths came faster. There was nowhere to go if we couldn't get in. Come on. Answer, I thought. My chest felt tight and the crush of distant voices hammered at my temples. An unseen speaker crackled into life delivering a short burst of white noise followed by a man's thin, distorted voice.

'Hello, yes? Who is this?'

The man was breathing heavily, and there was no mistaking the rushed urgency and undertone of surprise. I sighed and Grace turned to me and breathed a smile. Despite the relief, my whole body felt in a state of imminent collapse.

'We want to know if...' began Grace, but she shook her head and her voice failed her.

'It's Joel Durand,' I said, leaning forward. 'Henri Durand's son, can you—'

The static buzz from the intercom cut out. I turned to Grace and then looked back up at the speaker. I reached up, and despite the stabbing pain, jammed my finger on the button, pressing it again and again. The lens of a camera above us moved.

'Hello, hello? Come on, someone... answer.' I knew that I couldn't hold it together for much longer.

'Enemies of the people,' chanted Mum.

Grace's head fell forward. 'Please... Dad.'

'All for nothing,' said Sophie.

A white-hot rage surged through me, but Sky spoke before I had a chance to.

'We need to get away from here. I think things are about to kick off. Something big is happening in the square and I don't want to be around to—'

A loud, electronic buzz came from somewhere near the edge of the door. It clicked open. The intercom barked at us.

'Push the door. See you're not followed.'

'Oh my god,' said Grace.

Sophie shook her head. I pushed the door, trying not to let the rush of emotion overwhelm me. Inside was a dark corridor lit by dim, wall-mounted lights. The walls themselves were wood panelled and covered with a mosaic of pictures and photographs. Warm air rushed out to meet us.

'Are you coming, Mum?' I said.

She looked at us and then back at the door leading to the street.

'Mum,' said Grace. 'Please.'

Mum lowered her eyes before raising them and studying each of us in turn. Conflicting emotions played across her face before her jaw became still.

'I can't leave you again,' she said. 'Alright, I'll come with you, but if your father *is* here, I've got nothing to say to him.'

Mum allowed herself to be ushered through the doorway and into the quieter space but kept looking back the whole time. Her eyes were wide, as if she could see things that we couldn't. What had happened to her? I thought. I didn't know how to help her. Grace took Mum's arm and we moved along the corridor, transfixed by the images on the walls.

'Can I come too?' said Sky.

'What?' I said. 'Of course you can. Come on.' I put a hand on her shoulder as she walked through. Sophie stood on the threshold, in the cold.

'I don't suppose I fit in with your plans, now?' she said.

I looked down for just a moment and then back up at her. I breathed out.

'Sophie, don't be ridiculous,' I said. 'Come on, you're safe now.'

She wound strands of hair around her fingers.

'It's your choice, no one's forcing you.'

The intercom sounded. 'Come in and close the door.'

Sophie put both hands over her face and pulled them up and over the top of her head. 'I'm just so... oh, god. I just don't know what to think any more.'

My mouth opened to speak, but I was out of supportive and significant things to say. 'Just come inside,' I said, hot anger surfacing again.

I saw resentment and fear in her eyes as reluctant steps took her past me and onto the dark wood floorboards. I checked outside and pushed the door until it clicked. I breathed out. Grace's voice echoed from further down the corridor. We walked. My fingers throbbed in the unexpected warmth. I tried rubbing the blue out of them.

'There are stairs here at the end,' said Grace. 'Do we just go up?

'Yeah, I guess so,' I said, trying not to shout, but wondering where the person we spoke to, was.

We congregated at the bottom of an ancient set of solid-looking wooden stairs that ascended in a geometric spiral.

'This place is really old,' said Sky.

There was an overpowering smell of old books and polish.

Mum's eyes flickered, and she looked as if she was walking on nails. 'Where are we going?'

I took her hand and pressed both my hands around it. 'Come on.'

We climbed the stairs. Whoever was waiting would be aware of our progress. Our eyes strained upwards. Half landing followed half landing as the stairs ascended with only periodic wall lights illuminating the way. Sombre wood panelling added to the sense of antiquity. We arrived at a larger, more modern-looking anteroom with a wide metal door at the far end. White, with no discernible features, our footsteps echoed between the cold ceramic surfaces.

'This is some place,' said Sky. 'My dad said it was impressive.'

'It's hard to believe we're in the city,' said Grace.

Something clunked behind the white door. Metal on metal. A scraping sound followed the slow turn of a lock. The door moved inwards a fraction and then in one flamboyant manoeuvre, swung wide open. A new light picked out our dirty, tired faces. My heart thumped in my chest. Mum placed a hand just below her throat. Grace squeezed my arm.

A woman stood framed in the doorway. She seemed the embodiment of calm and sophistication. From her carefully plaited dark hair to her effortless black top and trousers, she was Paris, Milan and Madrid. She looked down at the screen in her hand and then scanned each of us with a brief, measured look. Her smile only wavered when she looked at Mum.

'Welcome. If you would all like to follow me.'

20. Library

Sky was the first to move forward, but I put a hand on her arm. I looked directly at the dark-suited woman.

'What's going on?' I said.

She pressed the screen to her chest and shifted from one foot to the other. Her head tilted to one side. 'I think you must all have been through a terrible ordeal. Please come this way; we have food and somewhere you can rest.'

Grace took a step forward. 'Is Dad here?' she said. 'My father—is he here?'

Apart from the merest flex in the corner of her mouth, the woman gave no indication of an answer.

'Come,' she said.

I nodded. The woman walked in front of us, her heels making a dull tap, tap on the hardwood floor. I turned as the door clicked shut behind us, the mechanical sound sucked up by the deep silence of a magnificent, high-ceilinged room. There were books—lots of books, stretching from floor to ceiling in rows of labelled shelves. The smell of cedar mixed with the fusty damp of old leather. Only Mum seemed unmoved by what she saw.

'This is awesome,' said Sky.

Sophie moved with deliberate steps a short way behind us.

The woman raised her hand. 'Stay with me, please, and don't touch any of the books.'

I wondered if she knew of the chaos and anarchy that was going on a few hundred feet away? She stopped beside what appeared to be a blank wall and faced us. Her face relaxed, and any pretence of social niceties disappeared.

'You must understand that what you are about to see, are about to learn, you cannot under any circumstances repeat to an outside agent. Do you understand?'

I nodded, as did Grace and Sky. Mum stared at the woman without blinking.

'Do you understand?' said the woman, glaring at Sophie.

Sophie nodded.

The woman pushed her shoulders back and stood up very straight. 'I am Jessica Dollond-Smith, head of public relations for the... well, he can tell you himself. Follow me.'

She led us through a rectangular opening into a dimly lit space filled with the sound of tapping and muted conversation. Mum didn't move.

'Mum?' I said. 'Are you coming?'

Mum nodded her head in a slow repetitive acknowledgement. 'That's her,' she said.

'Sorry?'

'JDS.'

Mum wasn't listening. I took her arm, and we shuffled to catch up with the others. Along both sides of a long, narrow room on small neat desks were lines of computer screens. Behind each one, with their backs to us, were men and women. They looked ordinary enough—regular clothes and some not much older than me, but there was no mistaking the intensity with which each engaged with their screens. Eyes sparkled in the shifting blue light. No one looked up or acknowledged us as we filed past. A young woman, seated near the middle of one of the rows, reached for a mug. She lifted it to her lips without looking away from the screen. I caught images of street corners, shop frontages, people.

'This way. Please don't disturb them.'

At the far end were two frosted glass panels that floated to one side at the merest of touches from our host. She stood to one side, tapped at her screen and dipped her chin.

'Please, come in.'

We entered a much larger room, which, with its mood lighting and tasteful furniture, felt just like a lounge bar or private members' club. There were chairs of all shapes and sizes arranged informally around the room and several small tables with magazines and drinks covering them. Between two heavily curtained windows, pictures adorned the walls. People of all ages were sitting, standing, talking, but as soon as we entered, the buzz of conversation stopped. All eyes turned to us.

'Oh my god,' hissed Grace. 'That's Mr Andreas, over there.'

Our Headteacher, or maybe former Headteacher, was sitting in a chair near the window, a laptop open on the table in front of him. He didn't acknowledge us. Instead, he adjusted his tie and resumed whatever he was doing. The whole setup was surreal. The pain in my side seemed, right then, to be the only thing I could rely on.

A door opened at the back of the room, and a man stood in the doorway. Smartly dressed with a dark shirt and unbuttoned jacket, I almost didn't recognise him at first. Even at that distance I could see the distinctive badge on his lapel. It was Dad. Something like liquid joy coursed through me, right from my toes, up through my back and to the hairs on the back of my neck. Mum was crying, huge sobs that convulsed her. She stood, staring, her arms at her side. There was no attempt to wipe away the snot and tears.

'Why, Henri?' she said. 'Why? Just tell me.'

Wide-eyed, Dad's mouth fell open. I'd never seen him look so shaken.

'Darling, what on earth's happened to you?' he said. 'I told you not to go.'

Jessica Dollond-Smith extended an arm. 'Please, Mrs Durand, you will be more comfortable in Mr Durand's office.'

'Get your hand off me,' said Mum.

Miss Dollond-Smith looked like she'd been stung. We started to move, but Grace ran forward and threw her arms around Dad.

'Dad. Oh, Dad.'

He kissed her, but his eyes were on Mum. She stood motionless and returned his wordless scrutiny.

'Come,' he said.

With his arm around Grace's shoulder he led us into a smaller mini-library. Dark wood panelling covered three walls with a fourth devoted entirely to shelves bursting with books of all colours and sizes. In front of an old fireplace a giant desk, littered with papers, screens and mugs, dominated the room.

'I'll leave you alone, Henri,' said Miss Dollond-Smith.

Mum's head turned like a whip towards the woman in the doorway.

'No, Jessica,' said Dad. 'I'd like you to stay.'

She gave the smallest of nods and closed the door. Adjusting her jacket and clutching her screen to her chest, she looked everywhere except at Mum. Mum's eyes held Dad in an icy stare. Something important had happened, but I wasn't sure exactly what it was. Dad smiled and came over to me. It was the smile that made me feel warm all over. Safe. He put his hand on my shoulder and we hugged. For a brief sliver of time there was nothing else but that moment. He looked into my eyes, moving his head to maintain the intimacy.

'Son, I can't tell you how good it is to see you,' he said. 'How did you find me? You are supposed to be safe at school.'

'Change of plan,' I said. I winced and instinctively looked down.

'You're hurt,' said Dad. 'Who did this?'

'I had a run-in with the school bully.'

'But you're okay?'

I nodded. 'It's nothing.'

'Okay. If you're sure?'

Dad turned to Sophie and Sky.

'And these are your... friends?'

'Oh yeah, this is Sky, and this is Sophie.'

'Sophie from school?'

'Er, yeah, how did you...?'

'Come on, son, I was young once, too.'

'I guess so.'

Sophie forced a smile but she looked as if she would rather have been anywhere but there.

'And Sky, wasn't it?' said Dad.

Sky nodded.

I touched Dad's arm. 'Dad, we need answers. We want to know what's happening.'

'Yeah,' said Grace. 'What's going on?'

'What is this place?' said Sky.

'When are things, like, going to get back to normal?' said Sophie.

'Yes,' said Mum, her voice dripping with sarcasm. 'Why don't you tell them everything, how you repaid the country that has given you so much.'

Dad's smile vanished. He silenced us with a raised hand and took a deep breath. 'You have many questions, of course you do, and I will explain everything. But first, would you like a hot drink, maybe some food?' He nodded to Jessica Dollond-Smith.

'I must talk to your mother.'

Mum snorted. He walked over to her, reached out and took her hand. She looked away.

'Jenni, please,' he said.

She turned her head towards him. Her bottom lip quivered. 'Everything we worked for, Henri. Everything we believed in,' she said. 'This life, our kids—all a lie.' She pulled her hand away from his and rubbed it as if to remove some stain.

'Can't we do this in private?' said Dad.

The veins in Mum's neck bulged. 'This affects them. It's their future, they have a right to know.'

'Has there really been a coup?' said Grace. 'Or is it just a hoax?'

'Yeah,' said Sophie. 'And who's the mystery guy behind it?'

Mum breathed out, lifted her chin and her mouth curved downwards. She sniffed and wiped her eyes. She looked at us and then at Dad. 'Go on, justify this to your daughter.'

Dad's eyes darted to each of us. I felt a dropping sensation in my gut. He took a deep breath.

'Alright,' he said. 'You deserve an explanation.'

21. Alternate Reality

'I haven't been telling you the whole truth,' said Dad. 'I mean, about my life, about what I do.'

He rooted in his pocket and took out a lighter, rolling it in his hand.

'This is harder than I thought,' he said. 'This place, these people...' His hand swept in a grand arc. 'Are part of a movement to stop the malign force that we know as Brexit.'

'So, Joel was right...?' said Grace, her face beginning to register unease.

'Are you part of this Temporary Administration?' I said.

Miss Dollond-Smith cleared her throat and looked down at the floor. I glanced at Mum. She shook her head and clasped both hands together. I could feel her anger—it was a living thing, radiating from every pore.

'You have to tell them, Henri,' she said.

'Well, yes, I—'

'It's a simple question,' said Grace. 'Are you involved with this coup?'

'Well, I wouldn't call it—'

'So it *is* true,' I said. 'Oh my god. Dad, they're calling you a traitor.'

'Why didn't you tell us?' said Grace.

Sky and Sophie both talked at once. The air was thick with accusations.

'I warned you that this was a bad idea,' said Miss Dollond-Smith. She walked over to Dad and stood at his side. She spoke with imperious confidence. 'We will not stand by and watch this country destroy itself, and everything that it has accomplished since the end of the last war.'

We stood in silence, our mouths open. The buzz of conversation from the next room filled the dreadful vacuum.

Sky took a step forwards. 'So you've helped start another one?'

'You are out of your depth, young lady,' said Miss Dollond-Smith. 'This is a provisional arrangement until fresh elections are held.'

'You're the one he's been texting, aren't you?' said Mum, looking directly at Miss Dollond-Smith. 'JDS. Morning, noon, and night. Did you both think I was stupid?'

I looked at her, then at Mum. A rush of blood made my face burn.

'Dad?' said Grace.

'Quoi?' said Dad, through a choked laugh. 'Miss Dollond-Smith and I have had to work closely on this project, yes, but that is all. I can assure you, Jenni, that it's completely professional and it's ridiculous to suggest—'

The look on Miss Dollond-Smith's face froze the words in Dad's mouth. He tilted his head and frowned. She looked away but couldn't control her mouth, which rippled with uncontained emotion. Her hand moved over her eye and her fingers shook. Dad turned to Mum. He raised his shoulders but it was obvious from Mum's expression that it was already too late.

'Tell *her* that,' said Mum.

It was as if someone opened a window and all the heat was sucked out from the room. Staring at Dad, her lips tight and unyielding, Grace placed an arm around Mum's shoulder. A line had been drawn—a choice, made.

A brief knock at the door broke the spell. A well-dressed young guy with neat hair walked in carrying a tray stacked with mugs. 'They need you, Miss Dollond-Smith,' he said. 'It's urgent.'

Dad nodded, once.

'Thank you, Callum. If you'll excuse me,' she said with arctic detachment.

Mum waited until the door clicked shut. 'You lied to me, Henri—lied to us all. You could have talked to me. I'm your wife, for God's sake.'

'Look darling, I never meant to—'

'But you did,' she screamed. 'I'll never forgive you, never!'

Dad moved a step closer to her.

'Don't you dare touch me,' she said, raising her hands to shoulder level.

Callum clutched the tray and stammered his way through a sentence. 'Er, Mr Durand, sir, shall I come back?'

Dad hesitated and then seemed to welcome the distraction. He cleared a space on his desk. 'No, it's fine. Put them down here.'

Callum put the tray on the table and made a speedy exit. I steadied myself against the back of a chair. I wasn't certain that the ground wouldn't swallow me up at any second. In some ways, that would have been preferable to witnessing the disintegration of my family. Grace was at Mum's side, their arms intertwined. They both looked at Dad with contempt. He squirmed as if someone had pumped acid into his veins.

'Please. Jenni, Grace—you have to believe me, I—'

'I think you've said enough, Dad,' said Grace.

I'd never heard that tone in her voice before, as if Dad were something that had crawled out from under a stone.

'*I* believe you, Dad,' I said. My heart was pounding.

Another young guy, a techy type with bad clothes and glasses entered without knocking. He tapped at his screen as he walked and kept biting his top lip.

'Sorry to interrupt, sir, but you need to see this; you're not going to like it,' he said. 'The situation in the square is getting ugly and we're seeing similar reports from all over the country.'

'Thanks, Matt. What about the army?' said Dad. 'The power stations are still secure?'

Matt pushed his glasses back up to the bridge of his nose, glanced at us and then back to Dad.

'It's alright, you can speak freely.'

Matt shook his head. 'It's not looking good. Drax has fallen.'

'What?' said Dad, running a clenched fist over his lips. 'But that can't be right. I spoke to them just an hour ago.'

Matt looked at his screen again, struggling to control his voice. 'Sir, it's here in front of me, and some areas of London also have power.'

Dad turned and slammed his fist down on the table. 'I knew we should have had extra personnel around these critical sites, but no, they wouldn't listen. So the power is back on?'

'It looks that way, sir, but the other facilities are holding.'

'For now,' said Dad.

With one hand holding Grace's arm, Mum took a step forward and pulled me towards her. Her eyes narrowed and her mouth was a thin line. She turned to Dad.

'We're leaving.'

Grace's eyes met mine. Mum didn't see the quick shake of her head.

'Mum,' I said. 'I don't think—'

'That's a crazy idea, Jenni,' said Dad. 'I won't allow it. Whatever our differences you can't make them go out there again. It's madness; it's not safe.'

'Do you agree with your father?' said Mum. 'Maybe you want to stay with him?'

'It's not that,' said Grace. 'It's just that it's dangerous out there.'

'At least we're safe in here,' I said, touching Mum's arm.

Mum pulled away and Sophie muttered something.

'Stay,' said Dad. 'At least for a little while longer.'

There were fresh tears in Mum's eyes. 'Look what you've done, Henri, turning my own children against me.'

'Mum, it's not like that,' said Grace.

'Jenni, please,' said Dad.

Mum took a step back, pulled her hand roughly over her face and raised her chin. 'I need the bathroom.'

It was as if Dad were seeing her for the first time.

'Yes, of course,' he said, waving his hand. 'It's just off the main room, Matt will show you.'

'I'll come with you,' said Sophie. She studiously avoided eye contact.

Dad continued talking. Mum and Sophie moved towards the door. At the threshold, without turning around, Mum hesitated. Her shoulders flexed and I caught the almost imperceptible turn of her head. Her chest rose and fell and she walked through the open door closing it behind her. Dad put a hand on his desk. All colour seemed to have gone from his face. The door clicked shut and Matt cleared his throat.

'I'm afraid there's more news, sir.'

Dad blinked and shot him a look. 'Aren't you going to—?'

'I'm sorry, sir, but the... *main residence* in London is surrounded.'

'So? The asset isn't there.'

Matt lowered his eyes and shook his head. 'I understand that he refused to leave.'

Dad inhaled sharply and his face turned to stone. Only his mouth moved. 'Are you telling me...?'

'Yes... I'm afraid I am.'

'Can't we get a 'copter in there?'

'Too many drones, sir.'

'Dad, what's going on?' I said.

'It's too complicated, son. I'm under a great deal of pressure right now.'

I gripped my side, pushing down a sudden pain.

'Don't you care about us at all?' said Grace.

'I'm not a child, Dad,' I said. 'We've been through a lot today.'

Dad took a step closer and raised both his hands as if was carrying an invisible globe. Fingers splayed, they moved in synchrony with his words, each emphasis earning a more pronounced gesture.

'Joel, Grace—you'll find this out when you're older, but there comes a time when you have to follow your principles and...' he glanced towards the door. 'Put everything else to one side. Everything.'

'So Mum is dispensable?' said Grace. She took a step back. 'And us, too?'

Dad's face reddened and he pulled at his collar, running a finger back and forth along the inside.

'Non, mes précieux. She is everything to me; *you* are the world to me. Never doubt that.'

Grace wrapped her arms around herself. Her voice shook and began to disintegrate. 'They said on the radio that what you're doing is treason. Dad, that's really serious.'

He walked back over to his desk and picked up a glass paperweight. Twelve five-pointed stars glinted within it as he turned it towards the light.

'If that's your definition, then yes, it is. But I had to play my part. I couldn't stand back and watch this country being destroyed by these right-wing monsters. All this is for the good of this country, the country I love and call my home.'

A high-pitched repeating sound came from a wall-mounted unit. It flashed red in time with the sound. Miss Dollond-Smith ran in. 'That's the main door; the camera shows two persons exiting the building. It's your wife and the blond girl.'

Like a hawk, Dad's head turned to a small monitor on his desk. 'Oh, Christ. Who let them out, there are strict protocols—'

'In case you hadn't noticed,' said Miss Dollond-Smith, her eyes flashing. 'The loyal, hardworking team here haven't slept in twenty-four hours, and they've got better things to do than follow members of your family around.'

A cloud of rage, despair and then panic crossed Dad's face. The repeating alarm stopped and he began to pace, his hand clamped to his forehead. 'My wife is in no fit state to be out there.'

Miss Dollond-Smith tried to intercept him but he ignored her.

'Sophie's behind this' I said.

'Or perhaps she's had enough of being lied to,' said Grace.

Her voice was cold venom.

'This is all my fault,' said Dad.

'Do you think?' said Grace. Her face was harder than granite, darker than obsidian.

'It wasn't supposed to happen like this.'

Dad put both hands on his desk and his head fell forwards. I could hear his rapid, laboured breaths. He looked up. His voice shook.

'Son, I'm so sorry.'

He reached out to touch the top of my arm but I pulled back, leaving him standing, his hand frozen in mid air.

'I can't do this.' I said, shaking my head. I felt both hands tightening into fists. 'I love you, Dad. I wish I could be part of this, but I've got to help Mum.'

I ran towards the door, turning back for the briefest of moments. Tears were gathering in Dad's eyes and Grace stood open-mouthed. I'd made my decision. My legs carried me through the building and the pain was a thing in my side, something waiting for its moment. I wanted to hear Dad's voice, ordering me to come back, to sweep me up in his arms like he used to do and tell me that I was his precious boy. He must have prepared for a moment like this, when he would have to choose. He let me go.

22. Escape

The beast was back, with a vengeance. I could feel its talons pulling at my side. I pumped out quick breaths like an old steam train. In the narrow surveillance corridor I noticed that many of the seats were empty, the unwatched screens spewed out text and CCTV images. A young woman, her head buried in her arms over a computer keyboard, was sobbing. I ran as best I could, although it was more of speeded-up shuffling limp while holding my side. I heard every distant voice as Dad's—ghostly echoes saying they would do anything for me not to leave. Pull your self together, Joel, I thought. A shrill soprano voice from somewhere behind me screamed at me to stop, to slow down, to wait. Mum and Sophie's faces filled my mind but I pushed them away. I couldn't afford to speculate on how this might end. The thought made my stomach turn to liquid. On the stairwell I struggled to go down more than one step at a time, each drop a challenge. At the bottom the air was cooler. From behind me came the reverberant sound of feet and voices. I made my way as quickly as possible to the end of the corridor. Holding my side and dragging my foot seemed to lessen the pain a little. I looked up at the camera and made an *O* with my middle finger and thumb. Dad always used to do this when there was something that he particularly liked. There was a part of me that understood what he was trying to do, and if I was honest, even admired. The time of feeling powerless and disenfranchised was over. I had to face the world and what was happening, head on. I only wished I'd known earlier, I could have helped. Or would I have tried to stop him? Perhaps we were the cowards and he was the brave one. I pressed the release button and pulled the door open. The cold and wind hit me like a fist and took my breath away. I closed it a little. For a moment I didn't think I could do it, but I knew Mum and Sophie weren't too far ahead of me. I grabbed the handle and was about to pull it when a breathless figure arrived at my side.

'God, Joel,' said Grace. 'For someone with stitches you sure can move.'

I wanted to acknowledge the humour but my mouth failed to respond.

'Let's do this together,' she said, and squeezed my arm.

I nodded. 'Okay.'

I pulled the door open wide and we stepped out of the security and warmth of the recessed doorway into darkness and pandemonium. Everything was different, as if there was an energy—a collective sense of purpose. A river of bodies and noise moved inexorably towards the square. Mum and Sophie couldn't possibly have resisted that momentum.

'I can't believe this is actually happening,' said Grace, her breath bursting in vapour clouds. I stood on tiptoe and tried to catch sight of Sophie or Mum, but there wasn't enough light. There was lots of smoke and the smell of burning rubber and wood mixed in with seared meat and fat.

'Stay close,' I said. 'Take my hand.'

Grace's fingers curled around mine and gripped tightly. We stepped into the street, and with our heads down, crunched through the peaks of grey-coloured ice crystals. The sea of bodies kept out the worst of the cold. A tattooed punk girl knocked into me and I slipped and fell onto one knee.

'You okay?' said Grace.

'Yeah, I'm fine.'

The atmosphere was carnival-like but with an undertone of menace. This was definitely no longer a Remain rally and I didn't want to think about what might have happened here, earlier. I hoped that Stark's threats were just bluster. I shivered, afraid of what lay ahead and with my free hand, held my jacket tight around my chest. Grace stayed close, her hand maintaining a link to another world of family, friends and privilege. The noise ahead was getting louder—a mixture of shouting, klaxons and random explosions. A firework zipped up into the air, culminating in a gigantic burst of white light.

Grace pulled my hand and as I turned she pointed upwards. The sky was full with near-stationary drones. Like a swarm of insects they hovered before finding new positions with machine precision. A woman in front of Grace stumbled, recovered and turned around. She showed her teeth and a narrowed eye, the Union flag tattoo on her shoulder exposed. 'Sorry,' said Grace. The woman seemed on the verge of making something of it when the guy she was with pulled her towards him. 'Leave it, Roxy,' he said. He grabbed her arm and they were swallowed by the crowd. Around us the shops on either side of the road were smoking shells, with fires still burning in some. Clothes, boxes and paper spilled onto the street. We kept moving, shuffling, negotiating. Grace's face was rigid with cold and the freezing wind found its way through every gap in my clothing. The street ended with two stone pillars, each supporting solid porticoes that stretched off to the left and right like protective arms around the square. Before us, stretching for as far as I could see was a vision of hell. We stopped. Grace gripped my hand tighter still.

The huge square was alive with bonfires and the largest crowd I had ever seen in the city. The biggest fire stood right in front of the Council House and above it, licked by enormous flames, effigies burned, their charcoaled shapes twisted and glowing red and orange. I couldn't tell if they were real or not. Sparks and embers, carried by biting gusts twisted over the crowd. All the trees had gone, every single one. The ghastly light from the fires flickered over the assembled masses, turning their faces red, highlighting dark, clone-like eyes. There was a makeshift stage to one side of the main bonfire. Someone clutching a megaphone was speaking to the crowd, their distorted words echoing around the tall buildings. Fists shot up into the air and a red banner rose behind the speaker. As it unfurled, I read the words—black capitals on a red background: THE WILL OF THE PEOPLE. The crowd roared, a throaty, deafening assault on my ears. Light and fire burst into the night sky. The unmistakable crack of gunfire made us cower for a moment. Controlling myself, I scanned the crowd for anything familiar. Everyone looked uniform, nothing stood out. Mum, where are you? I thought. My feelings towards Sophie had sharpened.

'I can't see them,' said Grace, her hair haloed with red. 'Maybe they went the other way?'

I shook my head. 'I know they're here.'

'My friends,' began a voice from the stage. The speaker was some distance away and I couldn't see them clearly. I missed the previous person's introduction.

'My friends, I have news—momentous news.'

The crowd seemed to quieten. I could feel the unanimity of purpose, the shared ideals. It was intoxicating.

'Today, as you know, this country was attacked.'

A sound like a growling animal, but much worse, began around me. The man on the stage waved his hands up and down.

'Yes, I know. Cowardly individuals, supported by other traitors trying to undo the democratic will of the people.'

A chant began somewhere to my left and spread through the whole gathering: *The will of the people... the will of the people...* Chanting from the distant ends of the crowd overlapped until there was just a roar of sound. Fireworks exploded above us and gunfire ricocheted between the walls of deserted department stores. Grace pressed herself against me. Where were they? My stomach tightened.

'They tried to marginalise us, belittle our views, but we held out for what we believed in. We believe in democracy, in the sovereignty of the United Kingdom.'

People went nuts, jumping up and down in a frenzied euphoria. The speaker wasn't finished.

'Sections of the army and the police have remained loyal and fulfilled their patriotic duty. I can tell you tonight that power has been restored to London and many northern cities. We've got the bastards on the run.'

He continued to shout over the rapturous response.

'We'll find these traitors, we'll track them down and—' He paused. *'Well, what do you think we should do with them? Show them mercy, understanding? Give them a hug?'*

A guttural, unearthly sound began. It came from the backs of a thousand throats as a rasping cry: *kill them, kill them, kill them.*

'I can't hear you.'

It grew into an all-encompassing maelstrom, a tidal wave of sound. I looked around; the people in the crowd were like pre-programmed robots. Someone grabbed my arm and pulled hard. A middle-aged woman with long straggly hair and a grey parting looked me up and down. Her brow was tight and low.

'Hey, why aren't you joining in?'

I tried to think quickly. 'I'm trying to—'

She didn't let go of my arm.

'Hey, don't do that,' said Grace. 'Leave him alone.'

'What are you doing here?' said the woman, narrowed eyes scanning around her. Other faces, their lips still moving in close sync began to turn towards us. 'I think he's one of *them.*' She pulled me harder as I tried to wrench myself away.

The judge and jury tone in her voice chilled me to the core. Grace took hold of the woman's wrist and pulled her hand away.

'Get off him.'

There was barely time to think. I took a step closer and pushed the woman as hard as I could. She fell backwards, taking at least three people with her. The sharp stab of pain in my side didn't stop my adrenaline-fuelled leap sideways into the crowd, disconnecting me from Grace's hand. I could hear the commotion behind me spill out. I knew they would carry out their screamed threats if they caught me. Don't go too fast, I said to myself... slow down, just act natural.

'I'm here,' said Grace. 'Keep going.'

A jolting pain pulled me up and bent me double. I imagined the stitches unravelling, skin pulling apart.

'Joel, you okay?'

I had no breath and could only manage a nod. The whirlpool of people pursuing us seemed to have dissipated. I controlled my breathing and began mouthing the same words as all the others and shaking my fist for good measure. Grace joined in. The chanting mutated into a vicious roar that reached right into my gut. I didn't know whether I was hot or cold any more. More guns discharged and the drones over our heads moved with sinister purpose. We were much closer to the stage and I could make out the face of the man speaking. I'd seen him on TV. Dad always used to shout and go off on one when he came on, called him a troublemaker and a rabble-rouser. He was living up to both claims, his sweaty jowls rippling as he bellowed into the microphone.

'This is our chance to create a new kind of society. A just, fair society for the people of this country. We will close our borders, yes we will, and restore the primacy of our Christian tradition. The culture of the indigenous peoples of this great island will be retained and supported.'

We were putty in his hands. His words felt so plausible, so... right. How could you not believe him, support him, trust him? It was all rubbish, of course. I'd been listening to that thinly disguised xenophobia for years. Craning my head above the crowd, my eyes fell on a familiar shape moving towards the stage. The voice boomed again and the bonfires spewed ash and embers into the black, drone-speckled sky. I followed the shape and without averting my gaze started to move methodically through the crowd, *sorry* tripping off my lips again and again. Grace found my hand, her grip tight and unrelenting. The shape ahead did look like Mum but I couldn't see where she was heading. My heart began to pound. Their eyes fixed on the stage; people seemed to barely notice us. The noise, the smell, the atmosphere of blood and triumph seemed to consume their minds. I stumbled and a sour taste filled the back of my throat.

'Joel, slow down,' said Grace, her voice thin and distant.

The pain was suddenly sharp and demanded that I stop. Breath was tight in my throat and I felt hot and cold at the same time. We were at one end of the stage. The lights and PA system were dark except for the occasional burst of light from the bonfires. Standing a little way behind the figure on stage, thickset goons with dark clothes were looking our way. We squeezed past stationary people, their faces caught in the hellish glare of the fires. My smile seemed to appease the irritated glances as we secured our way through. 'Hey, stop pushing,' shouted one man, but I wasn't listening. It *was* Mum. It had to be. I started to push harder, not caring who was in my way. Bodies scattered. Something clawed at my shoulder but I shrugged it off. I let go of Grace's hand.

'*A new era,*' bawled the man on the stage, his beer belly poking through the jacket on his cheap suit. '*To reclaim what is rightfully ours.*'

Send them back, send them back—the malignant chant virused through the tightly packed crowd. I was nearly there, just a few more steps. Behind me, Grace was calling my name but I ignored it, pressing forward. Somewhere from the crowd in front of me I heard another voice—a male snarl, louder and more insistent than the others.

'Mum,' I shouted. 'Mum!'

But the figure didn't react. There was so much noise. The voice, again. I kept moving forward and reached out. My elation was short lived. I stopped. Sophie stood at the centre of a tight circle with Mum next to her. Sophie's head moved in all directions as if she was looking for a way out. Mum, in her still colourful top, stared ahead, expressionless, her arms at her side. Surrounding them and maintaining the integrity of the circle was a pack of identically styled youths: skin-fade hair, low-slung caps and tracksuits. The oily-looking characters caught the flicker of the fires, twitching and gyrating to some base rhythm. From the deep shadow two figures moved forward. My breath caught in my throat. One of them was Kyle. Cigarette in mouth, his sinewy swagger projected infinite self-confidence, as if he were born for this moment.

I relived seeing his face in vivid close-up as he jabbed the knife into my belly—I remembered the cold of the metal, his narrowed eyes and twisted mouth.

My legs felt like they wouldn't carry my weight. Emerging from behind Kyle, waving his arms around and staggering like a puppet with wonky strings, came Stark. His misshapen face was stretched into an unnatural smile. Whatever he was on was stronger than beer. My throat dried and my guts rearranged themselves. The noise and commotion confirmed my descent into something resembling hell. A body squeezed in at my side.

'Don't move,' hissed Grace. 'Be cool.'

'Have you seen—?'

She nodded and grabbed my arm with both hands. Her touch was instantly reassuring. 'There are too many of them.'

One nation, under God...

'Hey, yeah, bring it on,' slurred Stark. He stopped and glared at Sophie, his smile on pause. 'Hey, everyone,' he said, beaming again. 'It's Sophie, the lovely Sophie.' He went to put his arms around her but she pushed him off. He barely seemed to notice.

... reclaiming our sovereignty.

'Fuck, yeah,' said Stark, joining a massive cheer. His arms shot high into the air and he started clapping, turning in quick circles. He staggered and nearly fell over. Mum inclined her head towards the stage, seemingly oblivious to her immediate surroundings. I tensed and Grace reasserted the pressure on my arm.

'Don't,' she said.

Kyle ignored Stark's wild gesturing and walked up to Sophie.

'Hey, babe, didn't think I'd see you again,' he said. He lifted her chin with a single finger. She returned his stare. 'Thought you was with your friends?'

Sophie tossed her head. 'They're not my friends,' she said.

'Not even the guy I skenged?'

She hesitated for a moment. 'No.'

Judas. I felt the stale tang of betrayal in my mouth. We stood in the intermittent darkness. People moved behind us, pushing us forward; we couldn't stay unnoticed for long. Kyle's needling voice spiked through the malicious rant of the man on stage. A girl, her blue and white thighs taut on teetering heels, put her arm around him. As he roughly pushed her away, a bottle sailed through the air above our heads. Kyle moved the back of his nail across Sophie's cheek.

'If you dare hurt me,' said Sophie. 'Daddy will hunt you down and kill you.'

Kyle stepped back and put his skinny hand to his forehead. He mimed someone peering into the distance. 'Ooh, I'm shitting myself. But wait, where is he? Where is *Dad-dy*?'

His cronies laughed. There was a commotion behind me and something hit the back of my head—hard. I fell to one knee. Grace screamed. Powerful hands gripped my arm and a man's gruff voice filled my head.

'This, him?'

'Yeah.' A woman's voice, older.

It was like looking through a kaleidoscope—a jumble of colours and shapes. My legs felt as if they belonged to someone else and the pain in my side took a back seat to the throbbing lump on the back of my head.

'Well, look who's joined the party,' said Stark.

A shadow passed right in front of me. I tried to focus. I smelled sweat and perfume. Grace's cry brought me back.

'Stop it, leave him alone.'

'*...secure our culture...*'

'Hey you, lady. Yeah, you,' said Stark. 'Fuck off. He's mine.'

The grip on my arm and shoulder shifted and the woman stood with her back to me. Her hair was like a bale of straw above the cracked black leather of her jacket.

'Hey, listen, you little cunt,' she said. 'You don't know who you're—'

'I said he's mine,' said Stark, taking a step towards her.

There was a blinding flash and a deafening bang. We all ducked. My ears rang. Kyle alone stood tall, one arm held high. His bony fingers gripped a small stubby object. It wobbled in his hand and then it too, caught the light.

'He's got a gun,' I breathed.

'Oh my god,' said Grace.

Kyle's cronies jumped up and down like pagan devil worshippers and the hands holding me loosened their grip. Stark stood absolutely still, knees bent. He stared, transfixed by the gun. I could see Kyle's eyes. Framed by a straight, solid brow; they were black, fiery holes: windows into hell. Psychopath. The woman vanished.

'Keep going you fucking old witch,' shouted Stark, his voice consumed by an asthmatic cackle. He moved next to Kyle and put a hand on his arm. He pushed down and the gun pointed towards the ground. Kyle pulled his hand away.

'Back off, Starky, man. This is my show.'

The back of my neck felt slimy and warm. Grace touched my cheek.

'You okay?' she said.

'Once the borders are closed, we can rebuild this country.'

I nodded. She pressed her body close to mine, her eyes fixed on Kyle. He swaggered closer to us while his cronies tightened the circle. Face to face, he nodded to dark shapes moving behind us. I felt a hand on my jacket and a black-clad youth held Grace's arm. She struggled but the guy twisted something and I saw the look of pain riot across her face. My lips tightened and heat pulsed through my body, pushing down the pain.

'You, again,' said Kyle. 'The tough guy and the weird sister. Didn't expect to see you anytime soon. It's like a cosy reunion—one big happy family.'

He pulled Stark into the mix and leant on his shoulder. Stark looked as if a giant spider had landed on him. Kyle's mouth moved in a pastiche of a smile but his eyes radiated a cold menace. I felt as if I'd stepped into quicksand.

'So, where was I?' said Kyle, turning and playing to his crowd. He put the barrel of the gun against his cheek and moved it backwards and forwards, provocatively following the line of his jaw. He wandered, almost casually towards Mum and Sophie.

'So, this is your girlfriend, sorry—*was* your girlfriend.'

'Just kill them,' shouted a skinny rat-boy sucking on a rollie.

'Yeah,' said another. 'Execution style.'

Grace's breath quickened. She struggled.

'Wait, let me turn me camera on,' said a girl with scraped-back hair.

Kyle moved towards Sophie. His lips curled and twisted and he pushed a strand of her hair with the barrel of the gun. She turned her head but I could see the whites of her eyes as she followed the metal cylinder, her shoulders and hands shaking.

'So, whose side are you on?'

Sophie lost it. 'I'm not a Remainer—I'm not. Just don't hurt me.' Her head fell forward, convulsed with sobs.

I felt a rush of emotions, among them, pity. How could I have ever felt differently? A low cheer rang out from the gang and Kyle nodded. He took a step to one side so he was facing Mum. The circle around them was contracting. Grace's jaw flexed.

'You a Remainer, then? You fucking look like one. She does, don't she?'

There were shouts and racist words. Mum moved her head very slightly and met Kyle's eyes.

'Is this Brexit?' she shouted, looking around. 'Well, is it?'

Her eyes were wild and Kyle stepped back. Don't Mum, don't, I thought.

'Your mother and father would be ashamed if they could see you now.'

I held my breath. Grace's chest began to rise and fall more quickly. Kyle spluttered and then roared with laughter. A ripple of sycophantic echoes followed until Kyle turned back to Sophie, his face like death. He jabbed her, hard, in the shoulder with the barrel of the gun.

'Who the fuck is she? No one talks to me like that.'

Sophie's eyes flicked to Grace. Kyle's head spun around and his top lip curled back like a dog, revealing crooked teeth. He glared at me, and then Grace.

'Aha.'

Kyle leaned into Mum and then looked to us. 'Is this your Mommie?' he said, in a baby-girl American voice.

Shrieks of laughter burst from the onlookers. Mum struggled and her voice was drowned out. I dug my nails into my palms and my breath pumped out between clenched teeth. I felt Grace's hand on mine. A curtain of smoke and fire climbed into the sky behind the stage.

'So, what *are* we going to do with you?' he said.

He put his arm around Mum's shoulder.

Stark moved forward. 'Hey, leave her, man.'

Kyle pushed him and Stark fell backwards onto the floor.

'I'm warning you. My show, my rules.'

The ground seemed to move, as if the molten core of the earth was pushing towards the surface. I could feel the pressure under my feet; feel the power of the molten lava. He moved the gun over the front of Mum's body.

'Nice tits, though.'

Stark was on his feet. He grabbed Kyle's arm. Grace screamed, broke free and launched herself forward. I watched in slow motion as her taloned fingers clawed at the burning air. She was a Black avenger, a dark eagle intent on revenge. Her wild, animal cry cut into my brain as I recovered and moved forwards in her wake. Kyle's mouth opened, betraying confidence, surprise and then fear. Stark pulled Kyle's arm away from Mum. Grace swayed from side to side as powerful muscles pushed down on the rising earth.

There was a sound, the most terrible sound I had ever heard.

Fire.

Screaming

Vibration.

The lights in the square came on.

23. Aftermath

'Just raise your shirt, please.'

The doctor's voice was business-like, matter-of-fact. She was a new one, but there couldn't be anyone in the facility that didn't know who I was. I lifted one side of my itchy, utilitarian shirt and she leaned in, pressing the top of a small penlight. Her fingers were cool and I enjoyed their gentle pressure around the wound.

'Mmm, yes, this all looks fine.' She was concentrating. 'The infection has gone and the stitches could come out tomorrow.'

She stood up, clicked off the light and walked over to a small sink in the corner. She elbowed the water tap into life and washed her hands. The treatment room was small and completely white, including the trolley I was sitting on. White cupboards, white shelves and empty white working tops. I guess they didn't trust me with anything on display, just in case I decided to grab a sharp object and do something stupid. I'd been told I was 'low risk', but with people like me 'you can never be too sure', I'd heard someone say.

'And the headaches, they've stopped? It says in your notes you received a minor concussion from a blow to the back of the head.'

I didn't want to think about it, didn't want to go there.

'Yeah, I'm fine.'

On the other side of the frosted glass door I could see my escort shifting position. I loved euphemisms. He was a guard and I was a prisoner. If I challenged anyone, I was met with sympathetic smiles and told that this was 'all for my own good.'

'Okay then,' she said, all in one big breath. 'Thank you, Joel. You can stand up now.'

She moved a curtain of jet-black hair off her forehead and managed a smile. I didn't reciprocate. I felt as if I might never smile again. She glanced towards the door.

'For what it's worth, I—'

The door opened and her mouth snapped shut. The escort, a thickset man with five o'clock shadow and a black uniform, stood in the doorway.

'All finished?' he said, looking at his watch. He clearly wanted to be somewhere else. He never spoke directly to me and I didn't know his name. The doctor cleared her throat and nodded.

'Yes. I've completed my examination.'

Her eyes darted to me and then back to the man. She gave a fleeting smile. The escort didn't acknowledge her reply. He glanced in my direction, jerked his head to one side and placed one hand on the open door. I pulled my shirt down with both hands.

'Thanks,' I said, and walked over to the man, offering him both wrists.

He snapped the cuffs around them in a well-practised manoeuvre and took my arm.

'Is that absolutely necessary?' said the doctor. She seemed to make a point of not looking at me.

'Rules,' he said, his voice low and disinterested.

I tried to imagine what his family were like, where he lived. I had to keep thinking, to keep concentrating.

'Yes, I imagine so,' said the doctor. 'I will see you tomorrow, Mr Durand.'

She must have seen the look on my face. The corner of her mouth moved.

The hospital wing was the only modern bit of the facility. The rest of the detention centre felt exactly like one of those old-fashioned prisons I used to cast sideways glances at on the TV. Ornate and colourful stone floors linked white-tiled walls and tall metal-framed windows with terracotta sills. It smelled of boiled vegetables and disinfectant. The only views were of the cobbled quadrangle where inmates were allowed to exercise for an hour a day. Talking wasn't permitted, so I wasn't sure what other people were being held for. The graffiti in the toilets told another story. Repainted every day, messages and statements remained in situ for a time. *Never surrender* was a favourite, as was *solidarity*. Threats of death and retribution to particular individuals were scratched in deep grooves in the soft stone.

Our footsteps echoed on all sides. In truth, my soft, non-lace slip-ons made more of a shuffling sound so it fell to the escort's beefy brogues to dominate. His mobile pinged, and he rooted for it in his back trouser pocket. A woman, her head down, walked past us in the opposite direction. She had a nasty bruise on the side of her face, and her eye was almost closed. Her hands were tied in front of her. The uniformed security guard at her side was an older woman with a pot belly and grey hair in a tight bun. She nodded at my guard. He ignored her. I felt as if I barely existed.

'Come on, keep moving,' said my guard. This was the first time he'd addressed me directly.

My leg still dragged a little, accustomed to compensating for the tightened skin just above my hip. I counted the light fittings on the elaborately decorated ceiling—one, two, three. I knew there were seven, but I couldn't help myself. I had to be sure. We turned left at the big four-corridor intersection, onto D wing, as announced by the elaborate Victorian ceramic scrollwork above the arch.

My room was close. Already I could feel the first stirrings in my stomach, the familiar tingling sensation in my chest and the leaden, crushing feeling. Breathe, I told myself. Breathe. I thought of her. If I closed my eyes, I knew I would see her. Don't. Just don't.

'What?' said the escort, looking up from his phone.

'Oh, nothing,' I said. 'I was... it's nothing.'

He snorted and looked down again. I stopped and he kept on walking.

'It's here,' I said.

He turned around and looked at me, in the way you would look at a fly or some other insignificant insect. He breathed out and walked back towards the heavily painted blue metal door in front of me. The digital key was the only concession to technology in this section. The door clicked open and I must have hesitated for a moment too long. He kicked it, causing the door to swing inwards on rusty hinges. He uncuffed me. I swallowed and walked into the centre of the small space. I stood quite still. Distracted by beams of sunlight streaming in through the high, square window, the door slam behind me sent my heart racing. Stay calm. Stay calm.

I looked back up at the squares of sunlight on the white wall. Too high to see out of, the window at least offered some connection to the outside. I didn't want to move. If I didn't move, then this might not all be real.

She was there again, in my head, trying to get me to talk. No, I didn't want to. She couldn't force me.

The room was hot and airless. The narrow plastic bed was too small. There was a desk and a toilet, but no pictures or luxuries. I had absolutely no intention of reading the Bible. A single light, in a round, crystal glass shade burned in the distant ceiling. This weak light was no match for the majestic beams moving at light speed across my room. The grille in the door was the only way out. There would be no problem if I were the size of a rat. The small speaker in the corner opposite the window burst into life.

'Visitor for Durand. Visitor for Durand.'

My heart raced. A visitor? Me? The grille flew open.

'Visitor for Durand. Stand back.'

The grille remained open until I had retreated further into the tiny cell, then the main door clicked again. I rubbed my hands together, already sticky with sweat.

A woman I'd never seen before stood in the doorway, her smart blue suit and short blond hair gave her a TV-ready look. I didn't trust her.

'Good morning, Mr Durand,' she said. Her voice was professional, practiced. 'My name is Ms James... Eleanor, and I'm with the rehabilitation programme.'

This was the first I'd heard of her and her organisation. I kept my mouth shut. She smiled an awkward smile, turning a metal bangle on her wrist. There was a sweet floral smell.

'You have a visitor,' she said.

I looked around her to see who it was. The woman laughed—a laugh that didn't involve her eyes in any capacity. I hadn't heard the sound of laughter in a long time.

'Oh, no. I'm here to take you *to* them.'

'Right,' I said.

Her eyebrows rose. 'Try not to look so upset, Mr Durand. This is a good thing.'

Did she know what had happened? I thought. I'd had a heavily censored letter from Sky so it couldn't be her, and Mum was on another planet. There was only one person I wanted to see, and that was never going to happen. I felt the familiar pressure in my chest.

'I'm sorry,' she began. 'Please come with me.'

I may as well have been sleepwalking. I followed her out of the cell and to a new area of the prison. Her mouth moved constantly, and dull, muffled sounds reached my ears but made no impression. I moved my head up and down from time to time and this seemed enough to satisfy her, to sustain a momentum. On the other side of double doors we arrived in a brand new, brightly lit reception area. There were armed guards at the main door and cameras everywhere.

'Why haven't you cuffed me?' I said, as we approached a high curved desk. A young woman sitting behind it followed my every move. Her expression was a mixture of loathing and contempt.

'We wish to present a good impression, Mr Durand,' said Ms James. 'We are not the uncouth mob as so often portrayed.'

I could see what was going on behind the corporate smile. I wanted to smash my fist into the middle of her face. She looked into my eyes and her sophisticated smile disappeared as if the muscles to her jaw had been cut.

'Yes, well. If you will follow me, your guest will join us in just a minute.'

Guest? George Orwell had this lot to a T.

I followed her into an anteroom that was no more than a white cube with one wall made entirely of glass. A blind, adjusted for privacy, covered it from floor to ceiling. In the centre of the room stood a simple table with two chairs facing each other. A single camera dominated the ceiling. Light came from a strip that ran at ceiling height, all the way around the room.

'Please sit down, Mr Durand... Joel.'

My name on her lips felt like a violation. I looked up at the camera and pulled a chair back, its legs scraping on the shiny cream-coloured floor. Music was playing from somewhere. I hadn't noticed it at first. I felt as if I was part of some PR exercise. The woman sat on the edge of the table. She winced a smile at me and looked repeatedly at a small device in her palm.

'Sorry about the—'

There was a knock at the door. I swallowed, not daring to imagine who it might be. Let it be Dad.

'Come in.'

The metal handle moved downwards and the door opened. A young woman carrying a screen walked in followed by someone with their head down. I didn't recognise her at first. Her hair was different. Then she lifted her head and the light caught her face.

'Hello, Joel.'

24. Ghosts

A thump of blood pushed its way up from my chest into my head. The vessels in my neck bulged.

'Get her out of here,' I said, standing up and pushing the chair back. 'Why are you doing this to me?'

Sophie's hand went to her mouth. She looked at Ms James.

'Mr Durand... Joel—' she began.

'You can't make me talk to her,' I said. 'I have rights, don't I?' I looked towards the door. It was as if someone flicked a switch in my head.

The burly, stone-faced guard took a step towards me, but Ms James shook her head. Sophie's eyes brimmed with tears.

'I shouldn't have come. I knew I shouldn't have come.'

'Joel,' said Ms James, putting one hand around Sophie's arm and extending the other towards me. 'Won't you just—'

'Stop calling me that, and stop all this bullshit politeness.' I raked my fingers through my hair and walked in a tight circle. 'You've only brought her here because you want something from me. I've told you before, I want to see my mother and father.'

Ms James looked at the floor, but not before giving Sophie a conspiratorial glance.

'I can't do it,' said Sophie, bursting into tears. 'I just can't do it. Joel, I'm so sorry.'

'Oh shut up, you stupid girl,' said Ms James, her voice lower and her mouth an unrestrained sneer. 'One simple task.'

'I hate this,' said Sophie. 'I hate myself. If I'd done something, maybe Grace...'

I could see her moving between Mum and Sophie. There was no sound, only muscle and bone. I tried to make my mind look away, but my subconscious was in full control. Her hands reached Kyle and found their mark. His eyes closed as Grace's nails tore at his face. Sophie and Mum seemed to reach out in unison but drew back after the first bang. Grace looked as if she'd received an electric shock. She shuddered, and then the second shot did its work. I saw the flash and then Stark's face—mouth gaping and eyes blazing. Grace turned to look at me and then back to Mum, her hands already reaching for her stomach. Her head jerked back, and she started to fall. Sometimes love isn't enough.

Mum screamed—a wild, animal sound.

25. Spectacle

Chairs were arranged in a broad semicircle about five rows deep. The room was the one with *SOCIAL* above the door. I'd walked past it dozens of times but never saw anyone enter or leave.

'Take any seat,' said an overweight middle-aged man with a fixed smile.

Apart from the exercise yard, this was the nearest I'd been to my fellow detainees. The other big difference was that there were women, although our khaki clothes rendered us curiously sexless. No one spoke, but there was lots of eye contact and glances laden with meaning. I saw despair, fortitude and defeat written in pale, grey faces. A white, pull-down screen and a ceiling-mounted projector, its fan working overtime, dominated the room. I sat near the end of one row, next to a tall man with big hands. He only glanced at me, but long enough to convey a sense of deep hurt and melancholy.

Ms James strode into the room, her heels a brisk and commanding *clack* on the polished stone floor. She was dressed entirely in black and exhibited all the natural warmth of a Siberian tiger.

'No talking. Take your places as quickly as possible,' she said. 'Thank you.'

The shuffling and scraping of chairs stopped. I noticed that there were two floor-mounted cameras facing us. I couldn't imagine what they were planning, but a cold dread gripped my spine. Ms James put a fist to her lips and let her head fall forward. We watched in silence. Rapid footsteps sounded outside the room. The part-glazed main doors swung open and a man and a woman breezed in. She carried a screen, and he a clipboard. They both wore crisp, dark suits.

'Sorry we're—'

Ms James raised her head, and her look silenced the woman. She flicked her head, took a breath and clasped her hands together. 'Well, now that we're all here, maybe we can begin.' Her withering look sent the couple creeping towards the back of the room. She took several precise steps towards us, appearing to enjoy these petty displays of power.

'You all know why you are in this facility.'

She scanned each face, her expression a mask of calm superiority.

'Over these long months we have tried to rehabilitate those of you who wish to participate in the new order.'

Only the projector fan made a sound in response. She took a few more steps in the opposite direction, her eyes finding new faces.

'However,' she said. 'There are those who we cannot reach, cannot help. The ones who initiated the attack on democracy.' The mask appeared to slip a little, with something darker and colder taking its place.

She let the words sink in. A bit of me, a very small bit of me, wanted to challenge her, to stir the others into some sort of rebellion. I knew there was no point. Some of them looked down, shaking their heads, others stared forward, their faces expressionless. Ms James folded her arms, running long, red-varnished nails up and down the sleeve of her jacket.

'Today is the day of reckoning,' she said, a certain eager breathlessness to her delivery. 'The perpetrators have faced the full force of the emergency courts. Evidence has been heard and sentences pronounced.'

My blood ran cold. Who did she mean? Her tongue played on restless lips. They seemed almost unable to keep still, as if desperate to impart the next piece of information. She arched her back and her upper body tensed. Her chin moved upwards, and I felt the hard, detached judgement of her stare.

'There is only one outcome for traitors.'

The echo of Grace's question to Dad in the Library reverberated around my head. My eyes stung. The lights flicked off and the sudden darkness left Ms James's haughty image burned on my retina. I swallowed. The projector burst into life, and an image of the British flag filled the screen. Every captive face drowned in the intoxicating red, white and blue light. The man next to me couldn't decide what to do with his hands. He put them on his lap, under his arms, and finally placed them together as if he were praying. The flag rippled in a CGI wind and a disembodied man's voice began speaking in a drawling, professional tone.

'Hello, and welcome to London.'

The flag dissolved into a panorama above Europe, with the familiar outline of the British Isles far beneath. The camera descended, breaking through clouds, and suddenly we were above London and the Thames winding snake-like towards the ocean. It offered us a birds-eye view of water, Tower

Bridge and the Tower of London before the camera swept in, finally resting on a suited figure clutching a microphone.

What was this? I thought. I looked around. Other figures, more shadows than people, had joined us at the back. There were four guards at the main door and there was no sign of Ms James. I had a peculiar sensation, almost as if I'd lived this moment before. I looked back at the screen and at the man, his mouth moving. He was smiling and walked towards two massive wooden doors. Two Beefeaters in vivid red and black uniforms pushed them open as he approached.

'Yes, Ladies and Gentlemen—today is Justice Day, when the organisers of the failed coup are punished in accordance with the Emergency Declaration.'

The man didn't stop smiling; it was like a perverted TV game show.

'Follow me now to the historic centre of The Tower of London, where, throughout our great history, traitors have met their fate.'

Mutterings began all around me. A man shouted, and I saw, or half saw, someone move quickly towards him. There was a staccato exhalation of breath and then nothing more. The mutterings diminished to a faint sibilance. I could feel my breath, hear it rasping in my throat. I licked my lips, my mouth suddenly dry.

The camera revealed an enormous square surrounded by high stone walls. Only just contained within the fortress was a huge crowd facing a raised stage. Security guards maintained a cleared central corridor along which the suited figure walked. Behind the stage was a massive white backdrop with five words in bold, red capital letters: THE WILL OF THE PEOPLE.

I didn't want to be in that room, didn't want to see what they were so keen for me to see. The crowd was silent—waiting. The man with the microphone walked towards the stage, making a bad job of trying to look where he was going and also talk to the camera following him. As we drew nearer, the camera picked up more detail. Along the back of the stage stood a long line of people, all wearing the same kind of clothes as me. Behind every fourth person, a guard stood with a weapon drawn. At the front of the stage was a smaller raised platform with a beam above it, supported by sturdy-looking braces at each side.

I leaned forward, scouring the faces of the men and women standing at the back of the stage. The camera jerked around as the reporter neared the steps leading up to the platform.

'The people assembled here on this stage today,' said the reporter, looking sweaty and uncomfortable, 'are the ringleaders behind the plot to undermine our democracy, to frustrate the will of the people.'

He sounded as if he was announcing a half-price furniture sale. As the voice droned on, the gathered crowd began to move. Banners and fists poked above the sea of heads, and a rumble of voices stirred. Music played—a march, and a different camera tracked along the row of faces at the back of the stage.

I saw him. It was Dad. My Dad—on that stage. It was a dagger in my heart. He was the fifth person in, his hair shorter and one eye not quite open. I blinked away hot tears. The camera kept moving. Dad looked straight ahead with his chin up and his lips pressed tightly together. My fingers found the cold steel of the underside of the chair and I gripped as hard as I could until I couldn't feel them. I looked around the room. Everyone's eyes were on the screen. Air rushed into my lungs, and a cold film of sweat formed on every surface of my body. The camera moved on and Dad was gone, out of shot. I would have given my life for the camera to go back so I could see him one more time. An uncontrolled tremor began in my lips and threatened to engulf me. I should have guessed that they might do something like this, but the reality was a thousand times worse than I could have imagined. I was glad that Grace wasn't here to see this. I wanted to turn away, to disengage, but, like all the others, I continued to stare at the endless parade of broken faces. There were so many, some familiar, although I couldn't place them. I tensed, hoping not to see Mum. She wasn't among them.

The music stopped. In the near darkness of the room I could hear the staggered breathing of the other inmates. I shared their pain. I tried to swallow but my tongue stuck to the roof of my mouth. I wiped my face. A drum roll made me sit up in my seat. The British flag filled the screen again and dissolved into a closeup of the structure at the front of the stage. It began to rain. The tone of the voice-over changed and became a clumsy parody of the sombre, patriotic voice that traditionally accompanies Armistice Day ceremonies. In the middle of the platform, surrounded by armed guards, stood a man in full military regalia, his hands behind his back. A little to his left was a woman, her head bowed, black hair covering her face. The man was escorted forwards. Beneath the primitive construction a black-hooded figure waited. He held a rope, one end of which was attached to the beam above.

A dark realisation spread like poison in my mind. The military man was positioned under the beam and held at each side. The rope was moved until it seemed to come out of the top of his head. The camera moved in, and I gasped. A hissed murmur surged through the room.

'Sit down' shouted a guard, leaning in from the aisle. 'Sit down!'

I looked around.

'Yeah, you.'

I sat down.

It was him—the Prince. So, the woman must be... I began to shake. Every nerve, every muscle convulsed in multiple spasms that rampaged uncontrolled all over my body.

Around his neck was a noose.

'No!' someone further along from me, shouted. There was laughter from behind me. The camera closed in on the Prince's face. It was a mask of self-control. His lips parted and his eyes opened. He nodded, almost imperceptibly, and raised his chin. `````

'Oh my god, he's going to speak,' someone hissed.

'For fuck's sake, get on with it,' came a rough, disembodied voice from the back of the room. Someone a few rows in front of me was crying. No one tried to stop her.

'My fellow countrymen and women.'

The Prince's quiet, hesitant voice boomed and echoed around the high walls. Each word, each syllable was drenched with emotion. He cleared his throat, his arms tight behind his back. Rain bounced off his forehead and nose, his hair beginning to darken.

'I have failed you, and for that I am truly sorry. I love this country—this nation. I must accept full responsibility for recent events and ask that there is unity, after such deep division.'

He blinked and glanced towards the woman to his right. He raised his eyes and looked directly into the camera. His expression hardened, and words burst from his mouth.

'After what my wife has endured I could not stand by and—'

The sound cut out. There was a shout from somewhere off camera followed by a monstrous scrape and a deep thump. The view cut to a wide shot, and the Prince dropped through the floor of the stage before stopping abruptly.

Screams erupted all around me, mixed with cheers from the very back of the room. The crowd at the Tower went crazy as the figure in front of them, dangling from the end of the rope, twitched and jerked. The woman on the stage fell to her knees. Music played.

I tried to think of the future, to think of something to cling on to.

There was only darkness.

THE END

AUTHOR'S NOTE

157

Thank you for reading my book. I hope you enjoyed the rollercoaster ride! I was inspired to write 'The Will Of The People' following an incident that happened to a close friend, so this has been a very personal journey. Joel Durand's story continues over two more novels. Until the next time...

All my best wishes,

Paul K Joyce